Merle

A Jacques Forêt Mystery

Angela Wren

To Anne
Enjoy !

Best wishes

CROOKED
CAT

Angela
July 6th
2017

Discover us online:
www.crookedcatbooks.com

Join us on facebook:
www.facebook.com/crookedcatbooks

Tweet a photo of yourself holding
this book to **@crookedcatbooks**
and something nice will happen.

To my mum and dad,
both of whom are
very sadly missed.

Acknowledgments

Grateful thanks go to:

Green Watch Crew Manager, Dave Bastow, of West Yorkshire Fire and Rescue Service for his invaluable advice and guidance.

Daniel Hodson, Technical Support Officer, for his patience and his knowledge and expertise in the field of IT.

My writing colleagues who have patiently listened, and encouraged me, when the writing of this story proved to be difficult.

My editor and publisher, without whom this would not have been possible.

About the Author

Angela Wren is an actor and director at a small theatre a few miles from where she lives in the county of Yorkshire in the UK. She worked as a project and business change manager – very pressured and very demanding – but she managed to escape, and now she writes books.

She has always loved stories and story-telling, so it seemed a natural progression, to her, to try her hand at writing, starting with short stories. Her first published story was in an anthology, which was put together by the magazine 'Ireland's Own' in 2011.

Angela particularly enjoys the challenge of plotting and planning different genres of work. Her short stories vary between contemporary romance, memoir, mystery, and historical. She also writes comic flash-fiction and has drafted two one-act plays that have been recorded for local radio.

Her full-length stories are set in France, where she likes to spend as much time as possible each year. She's currently researching and working on the follow-up to *Merle*.

Follow Angela at **www.angelawren.co.uk** and **www.jamesetmoi.blogspot.co.uk**.

Also by Angela Wren:

Messandrierre (#1 in the Jacques Forêt Mystery series)

Merle

A Jacques Forêt Mystery

la fête des morts

It was the tightly scrunched ball of paper that captured the attention of Magistrate Bruno Pelletier. His trained eyes swept around the room, only glancing at the naked body in the bath, and came to rest once more on the small, ivory-white mass, challenging and silent against the solid plain porcelain of the tiles. He stepped over the large pool of dried blood, iron red against the white of the floor, and, with gloved hands, he retrieved the object.

Carefully prising the paper back into its customary rectangular shape, he stared at the contents and frowned as he read and re-read the single six-word sentence printed there.

Je sais ce que tu fais

After a moment, he dropped it into an evidence bag being held open for him by the pathologist.

all hallows' eve, 2009

toussaint – all saints' day, sunday, november 1st, 10.00am

At his desk in Mende, Pelletier was reading the initial report of the previous day's death whilst he waited for Jacques Forêt to arrive. The building was unusually silent and he was still smarting from the verbal drubbing his wife had given him for having to be at work. Very much aware that he was foregoing a chance to see how much his recently born granddaughter had changed and grown, he sighed and slumped down in his chair. Missing much of this precious time with his own children when they were young because of his work was something he now bitterly regretted.

He pushed his mind back to the scene of the crime when he heard the door of the outer office open and then click shut again. Jacques, his long navy winter coat buttoned against the day's chill wind, strode into Pelletier's room.

"I've brought coffee," he said placing two insulated silver containers on the desk. Discarding his coat on the back of a nearby chair, he sat down and smiled. "What does the pathologist's report say?"

"It's only a preliminary one at the moment, so it is hurried, and it doesn't tell me anything I don't know already." Pelletier pushed the thin file across the desk to his visitor.

"And you're sure you want me to look at this?"

"Yes. I know you're no longer on the force, Jacques, but yesterday you arrived at the scene just as I was leaving. You had a reason for being there, and I want to hear more about that. Also, I value your opinion as an ex-policeman." Pelletier removed his rimless spectacles and began to polish the lenses with his handkerchief.

Jacques glanced through the meagre number of pages searching for the single relevant line he required.

Death by exsanguination from a knife wound to the left wrist.

"And the estimated time of death is recorded as sometime after noon on Friday…" Jacques said out loud as he looked up from the file. "Well, that fits."

"With what?" Pelletier replaced his spectacles.

"I now work for Alain Vaux of Vaux Investigations. One of our staff has not been into the office since last Thursday, and there has been no explanation from her either. She was due in the office yesterday as well but did not turn up, nor did she make contact to let us know why she was absent." Jacques quickly flicked through the other pages and then placed the folder on the desk.

"Ah. But that does not explain why you were in that building in Merle as I was about to leave it."

Jacques bristled. "In part, it does. Her manager, Madeleine Cloutier, has a regular meeting on a Friday afternoon in Rodez and, if she comes into the office first, always leaves at about eleven, eleven-thirty at the latest. On Friday, she asked me to check on Aimée, her absentee team member, if she didn't come in after lunch. At around three-thirty I called her office number and it was switched to voicemail, and when I called Aimée's mobile immediately afterwards, it was switched off. When she didn't come in for work yesterday, I called her again, at different times and got the same result. I decided to visit to see if she was OK."

Pelletier narrowed his eyes and paused in thought "But we have no positive identification for the body as yet." He picked up his coffee and watched Jacques closely. "We know that that particular apartment on the first floor is rented by Aimée Moreau, but we are still trying to identify and locate her next of kin." Pelletier consulted his notebook. "According to the Concierge, she rarely ever spoke, and he last saw her about three weeks ago, and even then, he could not be absolutely sure that it was her as she was walking away from him."

"I can make an identification if you wish," said Jacques. "I've been working with Aimée for a few weeks now, and I'm sure that we will have details of the next of kin on file at the office." He relaxed back in his chair and rested his left ankle on his right knee.

"Ah. That would be very useful, Jacques, and I would be glad of your assistance, but I have to understand in detail why you thought it necessary to visit the apartment of a colleague. I am sure that your presence in the building, where an unexplained death has occurred, can be accounted for satisfactorily and that I will be able to eliminate you from the enquiry. However, just now I need to focus on you."

Jacques remained composed. "I understand that, Bruno, and had the situation been reversed I would be saying exactly the same thing to you."

Pelletier clipped the base of his cup on the edge of the desk and some drops of coffee splattered pale brown spots across the open notebook in front of him as he set it down. "So, tell me about your connection with the owner of the apartment." Retrieving his hanky, he hesitated and then repocketed it and shook the open notebook over the floor and let the drops of liquid slither off the pages.

"It's purely a professional one. I'm employed on a permanent contract as a Senior Investigator, working directly to Alain Vaux. His brother Édouard runs the sister company, Vaux Consulting. Both of these businesses, which operate independently in different business fields, but also share some services internally, form the privately-owned Vaux Group. Aimée Moreau is employed as an Assistant Consultant in the central project management team that works to Édouard Vaux. Her manager and the rest of the team are involved in a project to redesign the working practices, rebrand and refit the offices of a major insurance company located throughout the *départements* of Lozère, Gard, Averyon and Hérault. It's a substantial four-year contract with the possibility of further work in other *départements* in the regions of Midi-Pyrénées and Languedoc-Roussillon if this first tranche of the project goes well."

"And how long have you known Aimée?"

"I first met Aimée on Tuesday the first of September. My new contract of employment began on that day. But I did not actually have any close dealings with her until I was assigned my current investigation by Alain Vaux—"

"Which is?"

Pelletier's as sharp as ever, thought Jacques. He sat up straight and cleared his throat. "A delicate matter, so I must ask for your discretion."

The magistrate gave an almost imperceptible nod.

monday, october 12th,
three weeks earlier

Jacques flipped over to the last page and, whilst he could see the obvious downward trend on the graph, he failed to fully understand what the figures were supposed to be telling him. He placed the papers on the desk and sat back in his chair.

"I'm sure you've now realised why I have to act," said Alain Vaux as he nodded towards the document. "Those are the losses, month by month, compared with last year, up to the end of September. I discovered at Friday's board meeting that yet another contract, for which we provided a very competitive and compelling bid, has gone to another firm. I suspect it is C and C Consulting, and this isn't the first time they've picked up what should have been one of our projects." Alain brushed his hand down his tie and rested his forearms on the desk, fingers tightly intertwined.

"Surely you cannot be certain about whether a contract is to be awarded to you or not. Isn't that the point of the tender process? A fair route to find the most qualified bidder to undertake the work at the most economic price?" In the four-and-a-bit weeks that Jacques had been with Vaux Investigations, he had learned to never assume anything and to question everything. In comparison with some of the cases he'd handled in Paris, his work thus far had hardly been testing. There'd been the internal investigation involving minor theft, a couple of domestic cases that had been quickly resolved, and some background checking on senior managers in another company with which Vaux Consulting wanted to sign a five-year contract. Every case he'd handled had been well within his capability. But this new assignment was something completely different and he was beginning to feel uneasy.

"In principle, yes." Alain glanced through the fourth-storey windows to the building opposite. "But, you know, people talk. Sometimes unguardedly, and you never know who might be listening at those moments. Employees move from position to position and between companies, and why would you not use any helpful information that they may have." He shrugged as a pragmatic half-smile crossed his face.

Jacques shifted in his chair, frowned and stared at the wall behind his boss's desk. "Are you suggesting that someone, either here or within your sister company is leaking information to competitors?"

Alain rose to his feet and moved over to the windows. "No, not exactly. But there is something amiss. I've been running my own business for a over thirty years, and I know that my and my brother's half of the group are both clean. But I also know that some of our competitors do not have quite the same reputation as us and are not as fastidious as us in their business dealings."

Jacques scrutinised Alain's reflection in the glass. The watery grey eyes were cold and unblinking and the pale features emotionless and inscrutable. "I'm just an ex-policeman, Alain. You're going to have to give me a bit more to go on than a spreadsheet of figures, a graph and a gut feeling."

"An ex-policeman who is known to get his man, Jacques. That's why I employed you." He glanced at Jacques and smiled briefly "My brother, Édouard, runs a tight organisation, as do I. But someone, somewhere is... I'm not sure what is happening but the result is that we are losing contracts. Someone is working very hard to steal our market share, and I don't believe this is anything to do with a genuine shift of business to a better competitor. What has been happening to Édouard is now affecting my half of the group. I've just lost a contract with a company that I've been associated with for six years. A couple of weeks ago, it

9

was a contract with a medium-sized employer that we had supported for two years only. It's the same pattern. A relatively new contract disappears from the books, but the income stream can be replaced a short while afterwards with relative ease. Then a more established contract disappears and so it goes on. It's the pattern of the losses that makes me suspicious. If the losses here at Vaux Investigations accelerate over the next few months along a similar curve to that graph, then we will be staring bankruptcy in the face." When he turned towards Jacques, his brow was furrowed and his colour ashen and weary.

"All right. I think we start with previous employees. Anyone who has left either part of the organisation within the last few months. I will need a list of names, last known addresses and the reason for leaving. Once I've got that, I will first make enquiries about those who were sacked, whose contracts were ended early or not renewed. I'll need access to personnel files; detailed information for all the lost bids and that must include all confidential documents. Also, if your suspicions are correct, I cannot ignore current staff who have been in continuous employment since you and your brother first noticed that there may have been a problem."

Alain nodded and returned to his desk. "I'll authorise all of that but there are conditions. I want you to start by looking at Vaux Consulting. If there is anything to find, it will be there. I also want you to work there. I want you to observe, at a day-to-day level, what is going on. To facilitate that I've agreed with Édouard that you will work with Mademoiselle Lapointe and she has allocated a spare desk to you in the operations area. But you will report your findings, all of your findings, to me and to me alone. We will tell everyone that your role is to look for efficiencies. The permanent workforce is already aware that we may be looking at reducing our overall staff numbers at all levels. So, placing you there will not surprise them."

Jacques thought for a moment and then shook his head. "I can't agree to that. If you want me to conduct an internal investigation of this nature, then you have to let me handle it in my own way. In addition, the workforce across the group must already know my background and your ruse will not be believable. Also, you need to remember that I've worked undercover on major police investigations whilst I was in Paris and this is not a time for subterfuge. And no one can be excluded from consideration, Alain. No one. Not even you."

Alain glared at Jacques. "If the problem is an internal one, won't that alert the one person we are trying to identify?"

"Yes, it will and that can only work in our favour. He or she will feel under pressure and is then likely to make mistakes."

"Tread carefully, Jacques."

The last instruction rankled, and Jacques took a deep breath. He was always careful. Always had been, apart from that one night around the Porte de la Villette in the 19th *arrondissement*, and he'd paid the price since. Dismissing the mild, and what he finally decided was an unintentional, insult, he stood. "I'll see myself out."

Boulevard Théophile Roussel was teeming with traffic when Jacques made his way towards the pedestrian crossing. As he waited for the lights to change he stared at the four-storey building opposite that housed the sister company, Vaux Consulting. He couldn't help thinking how convenient the positioning was. It would be so easy to set up a covert watching and listening post if he needed to. But that may not be necessary; he'd have to wait and see how the investigation progressed. He smiled to himself and straightened his shoulders as he crossed the road.

Investigative work that can only get more and more interesting.

The pass for his own building allowed him admittance to Vaux Consulting. A security risk that he had already pointed out to both Alain and Édouard and, on a less formal basis, to the Head of Security for both sites. Still no action had been taken. He nodded to the security guard at the reception desk, a painfully thin young man in an ill-fitting grey uniform, who seemed out of place in his current surroundings. Jacques had wondered more than once why such a quiet and uncommunicative individual had been employed in a public-facing role, but had resigned himself to accepting others' decisions, even if he thought them misguided.

"*Ça va*, Luc? Is Serge in his office today?"

Luc nodded and mumbled his response. "Through there."

Jacques strode across the marbled lobby, tapped on the door marked *Sécurité* and walked in.

Serge remained at his desk as he always did. "Jacques, what can I do for you?"

"I'm making some preliminary enquiries in relation to an internal investigation, Serge, that I think you can help me with." He pulled out a chair, sat down and took his notebook from the inside pocket of his jacket. "A few facts that I just want to crosscheck with you first. All staff in this building have a pass that also allows admittance to the building across the road; that's still correct, isn't it?"

Serge nodded. "Are we going to revisit this issue again, Jacques, because I just want to remind you that the decision of the board was that no action would be taken."

"I know that. I just want to clarify the facts, that's all. So, everyone in the building opposite has access to this building, yes?"

Serge nodded again.

"And temporary staff have temporary passes that end with the last day of their contract. Is that still the case?"

"Correct." Serge watched Jacques make his notes.

"So, a temporary member of staff…if their contract were to be renewed on their very last day of service, would have to apply for a new pass, yes?"

"That's correct."

"And how long do you keep those applications?"

"For the whole Vaux Group, only as far back as when they moved into this building and the one opposite, that's about two and a half years."

"And I know the system for day visitors is different, but just remind me of the process, Serge."

"All personnel input the details onto a spreadsheet, which is held on the open access area of the office network, detailing all expected visitors for each day of the following week. We add them to the database and obtain a signature on arrival and issue a day-only pass. We sign them out when they leave. And we have all those records, too."

Jacques took his time making his notes to cover a broad grin that he could not stop from forming on his face. He drew a heavy box around the words 'office network' and 'open access area', adding after it the word, 'ANYONE'.

"OK, the appearance is that we have records of all expected personnel in the building at any one time. But what about people who stroll in? It would be quite easy for someone to arrive behind an existing member of staff who has a pass and just walk in."

Serge let out a sigh. "And we've been through this too, Jacques. The CCTV covers the entrance and lobby at all times. We handle that very effectively at the moment, and all unauthorised personnel are escorted from the building."

Jacques looked closely at his fellow employee. His dark heavy eyebrows were drawn together and his shrewd brown eyes were narrowed with the beginnings of impatience. He wanted to challenge him and point out that anyone within the organisation could legitimately allow access for a day to the most notorious criminal in the south-west if it was made worth their while.

"OK. Thanks, Serge, and I may need to access some of those records."

"Be my guest," he said as he swivelled around in his chair and nodded towards the bank of black metal filing cabinets lining the far wall.

Jacques took the hint and rose to leave.

"Just one question of my own before you go. This internal investigation... Do I need to be concerned or to take any action?"

Jacques frowned momentarily before replying. "No, I

don't think you need to worry at this stage, and I'm not yet able to decide if you need to take action or not." Before Serge could say anything else, Jacques was out of the door and striding across the lobby.

As he took the stairs to the fourth floor he let his mind wander through a mental image of a map of the security processes, noting pinch-points, open hand-offs and areas of risk. *Serge truly believes he has watertight security.* He grinned to himself and stopped, flipped his notebook open and stared at his jottings about the network. *We need to review the open access area.* Pocketing his book, he took the last few steps onto the final landing and let himself into the senior management suite.

Roger Baudin, the Finance Director, was in his office on the right, door closed. Through the glass wall, Jacques could see the company accountant, Roger, and his senior manager, all with dark looks on their faces as they huddled over their papers. On the left, the Operations Director's office was empty as usual. As were most of the desks in the large open-plan operations area. Next was the cavernous and empty boardroom on the right, and at the end of the floor, Édouard's suite of offices.

Unlike his brother, Édouard insisted on employing a personal assistant, and Mademoiselle Lapointe was everything her name suggested. Unusually tall for a woman, she was also angular in appearance. Her black hair, fading to grey at the temples, was always drawn tight at the back of her head and her intense dark brown eyes never missed a single detail.

"Monsieur Forêt, I've been expecting you." She rose from behind her desk and crossed the room to a small lockable cabinet. "Monsieur Alain telephoned and asked me to pass these papers to you." She handed Jacques three sealed courier pouches. "They are confidential and I must ask you to sign here, please." She placed the form in front of him and handed him her pen.

Jacques smiled at her. "Thank you, Mademoiselle Lapointe, and please call me Jacques."

"Anything else, Monsieur Forêt?" She removed her spectacles and placed them on the desk.

"Yes. May I sit?"

Mademoiselle Lapointe nodded and then remained motionless and stiff-backed waiting for his next question.

"Who has access to confidential documents for bids, Mademoiselle?"

"Myself, the directors, but only in relation to their own work area, some senior managers as required, and Messieurs Alain and Édouard."

"And does that include confidential contractual and financial information as well?"

"Naturally."

"So, all of these people can freely access all of those documents through the office network. Is that right?"

"Not all, no."

Notebook in hand, Jacques waited. "Can you expand on that, Mademoiselle Lapointe?"

"Some documents, especially those being put together for bids for work, are only available on the network to Édouard and Alain. If any of the other directors need access they have to ask me, and I allow them system access for the day or the week as required. We have tightened up on who can access that documentation since Édouard became concerned about the number of bids of ours that had failed."

Jacques nodded. "So, you can provide me with a detailed list of who has had access to which tender documents, is that correct?"

"Only for the last six months or so."

"OK. If you could let me have that information by email as soon as possible that would be helpful." He smiled as he tucked his notebook back into his jacket pocket.

"Of course, Monsieur Forêt."

Jacques stood. "Thank you. The name is still Jacques."

The slightest glimmer of lightness appeared in the corner of her eyes as Mademoiselle Lapointe turned to her computer, keyed in her login details and password and then continued with her work.

Jacques walked back to the landing and again took the stairs before making his way out onto the street and back to his own building and desk.

***

Crossing the Col de la Pierre Plantée, Beth Samuels began to relax and a smile gradually crept across her lips. She slowed the car and looked left to the distant heights of Mont Lozère and the stress of the two-day drive began to ease. Since her last visit in June the scenery had changed. The bright yellow clumps of the mimosa had died back to the colour of moss and the previously bright green grass, bleached by the relentless July and August sun, had turned to an insipid shade of straw. The familiar vast grey boulders remained strewn across the landscape, a pale contrast against the dark pines of the forest beyond. But that darkness was now beginning to be softened by the rich colours of autumn in the canopies of the many broad-leafed trees. Pulling her attention back to the road, she corrected the position of her vehicle as she began the short descent towards the village and the final few-hundred metres of her journey. From the last bend in the road, she could see the roofs of the village and the chateau ruins above.

Hmm… My temporary home. This time it really feels like I'm coming to…my temporary…no, my second home, perhaps rather than just coming back.

She took the next right and pulled up in front of the restaurant and the Salle des Fêtes.

Through the large expanse of window that stretched almost from floor to ceiling, she could see Gaston, the flat wicker basket that she knew contained a cheese platter in his hands, chatting to two businessmen. As she pushed the car door shut, she waved and walked in. Marianne immediately abandoned her task of clearing plates from an empty table and rushed across to greet her.

"You're back! Good; we've all missed you," she said as she kissed Beth on both cheeks.

Gaston, cheeseboard discarded on a nearby table, also kissed her. "Jacques's been moping. I think he's missed you." Stuffing his hands in his jeans pockets, he perched on the edge of the empty table behind him.

Marianne cast him a sharp-eyed glance. "Jacques's been fine, and does he know you are here yet?"

"Not yet, but he will do soon. He made me promise to text him when I got here. I was wondering if I could get a bottle of wine for tonight, Gaston."

"Of course," and he was immediately weaving his way through the tables to the bar.

"You look well, Beth. And I like the hair!"

Beth smiled. "That's something else Jacques doesn't know anything about yet… I just needed a change, you know and I…"

"It really suits you."

"Your wine," said Gaston as he presented her with a bottle of Limoux. "And it's on the house, a welcome-home gift from us both."

"Thank you… Strange that you should call Messandrierre my home… As I was crossing the col I had a similar thought myself."

Marianne grinned. "Good. We want you to think of us as family."

Beth glanced from one to the other as she tried to subdue and control an unexpected tear from making an appearance. "I think, perhaps, I already do," she said.

The bottle left on the passenger seat, Beth manoeuvred the car and drove the last few metres along the D6 to the chalet and pulled onto the drive. The outer wooden door was latched back and the black planter was in its usual place in front. She frowned as her gaze focussed on the hydrangea in the pot, the leaves wilting and the tawny-hewed flower heads shedding their petals.

"Jacques hasn't been paying you the attention you need whilst I've been gone, has he?" she said as she stood on the decking, fishing her keys out of her handbag and unlocking the door.

17

Jacques began sorting through the files from the pouches, and the additional ones he'd collected from the HR Director's office. All of the papers laid out on his desk, he brigaded the senior managers' documents and those of their assistants on one side and other staff, both past and present, on the opposite side. Picking up Mademoiselle Lapointe's file first, he immediately went straight to the back and started working methodically through the individual pages, making notes as he went along.

Eloise Lapointe had joined the company, aged twenty-eight, in 1983. Jacques looked at the photograph that was stapled to her application and studied it. Then, she had been a striking young woman, and he wondered why she was, apparently, still alone. He checked the personal details section again. She was single then, and it appeared, had remained so. *What a waste!*

Returning his attention to his immediate task, he noticed that her first appointment was as Édouard's Personal Assistant, a role that she still occupied. Again, he wondered why. She was obviously an intelligent woman, university-educated with a degree in finance and economics and over-qualified for the job that she did. Jacques frowned.

So why doesn't someone as smart as you have more ambition?

He jotted down some questions.

Leafing through the remaining documents in the file, he discovered that there was nothing out of place; her work record was exemplary, she had been paid various performance bonuses over the years, and there was only one request for compassionate leave in 1985 to arrange her mother's funeral.

A pain stabbed at the back of his eyes as he recalled standing at his own mother's graveside in Paris a few months earlier. He recognised that it was always going to be unguarded moments like this that would prompt him to acknowledge, and momentarily face, his grief whether he wanted to or not. He scraped his finger and thumb across his eyes and squeezed the bridge of his nose until the bone could absorb no more pressure. Glancing back at the request for absence in 1985, he read the details again but didn't bother to make a note.

He slapped the card cover of the file shut and dropped it back into the green pouch. The next on the pile was for Alain Vaux. A much larger and well-used set of documents to work through, and Jacques started with the earliest and made any appropriate notes as he went over the papers. There were copies of letters, notes about business awards, further qualifications and then, not attached to the tag or any other document, a torn sheet of pale blue notepaper containing what appeared to be part of a hand-written letter. It seemed to have been slotted in to the file as an afterthought. Everything else was in precise date order, but this was completely out of sequence. He removed it and slotted a folded blank sheet of paper in its place. He then searched through the rest of the documents looking for the envelope and the rest of the page, but found nothing. He turned his attention to the wording. The script was rounded and not French, of that he was certain. He placed it against the open page of his notebook for comparison and nodded.

"Definitely not French," he said to himself. Not really sure if it would have relevance to his investigation or not, he got up and photocopied it, just in case. Returning the original to its place in the file, he folded the copy and slipped it at the back of his notebook just as his phone rang with an individual and familiar tone that denoted the arrival of a text. *She's back.*

A wide smile spread across his face as he examined the final few documents and concluded that Alain's file contained nothing else of interest. It was soon deposited in the pouch. A glance at his watch and his next action was decided without conscious thought. He cleared his desk and left for the rest of the day.

tuesday, october 13th

"Thanks for the updates, everyone. We're in a good position. At the Stakeholder Group Forum on Friday, it became clear that this phase of the project is going to over-run. Which is a worry at such an early juncture." Madeleine Cloutier stared down the boardroom table and waited for the concerned murmurs to subside.

"But why?" Hélène Hardi pushed her circular black-framed spectacles up to the bridge of her nose. "I know we've another three and half years to get all this work done, Madeleine, but a delay now is sending the wrong message to stakeholders, senior managers and to everyone who's already worked so hard to meet the constant and demanding deadlines." A grimace sat on her round pale face as she waited for an answer.

"I know. But the first level IT design won't be ready, and getting the IT right is a critical foundation." Madeleine let her gaze travel across the faces of the assembled team as the impact of her announcement sank in. "I also want to make clear that the overall end date of this programme of work has not been adjusted and remains as April 8th, 2013. The training and implementation period also remains the same which means that phases two and three will be squeezed." Madeleine's clipped tones echoed around the still and silent room.

It was Hélène, with her strident voice and ingratiating tone, who broke the tension.

"Madeleine, that's placing an even greater risk on the IT work. If they're behind at this early stage, then squeezing the follow-on phase of work must be placing the whole programme in danger of failure—"

"I think the stakeholders and IT Director do know what they are agreeing to, Hélène." The edge in her voice was not missed by a single person present. Madeleine paused for a moment. "Any questions?" A dull shuffle pervaded the room as people began to close notebooks and collect papers together. "All right. Back to work, everyone. And please remember that everything I've said today is absolutely confidential. The next meeting is Thursday, in preparation for the Checkpoint Meeting with Édouard the following Monday."

Madeleine stood and checked her phone. Once the last of her team had left she closed the door and directed a winning smile at Jacques.

"Well, Jacques, you now know what myself and the team are trying to do. I hope that was helpful for you." She sidled down the room and perched on the edge of the boardroom table, her tight pencil skirt pulling across her thighs.

"Yes, thank you, but I need some details. You mentioned a Stakeholder Forum, but I'm not sure exactly who or what the purpose of this forum is?" Jacques sat with his pen poised to add to his notes.

"The Forum is the most senior authority for the whole programme of work. It includes the senior representatives from our client, so that's the Chief Executive, Deputy Chief, Operations, IT, Finance, HR and Estates Directors along with the appropriate counterparts from Vaux Consulting.

Jacques focused on his notes and continued to write. "And the purpose of the group?"

A flicker of contempt crossed her face. "They commissioned the work, and now that we – the project team – are in place and the scope of the work is defined and agreed, they steer and decide policy and make decisions on new policy issues as they arise."

Jacques continued to take notes.

Madeleine scraped her short, strawberry blonde hair behind her ears and, back straight, smiled at Jacques. "It's been a long time since Paris. How are you?"

"I'm very well, Madeleine." Looking her straight in the

eye, he pushed his chair out and moved to the other side of the table. "Today's meeting was useful background, thanks. I will still need to interview you as already agreed. It would be helpful if you could make every effort to keep that appointment."

"So very formal, Jacques. It would be nice to catch up outside of work, don't you think?"

Jacques studied her face for a moment. The brown once smouldering eyes now seemed cold and empty, yet he still recognised the winsome smile. "I'm with someone else, Madeleine. Someone I can trust implicitly. We'll talk on Thursday, as agreed. And we'll talk only about this company, the work and my current investigation." Without further hesitation, he collected his papers and notebook and marched out of the room. When he reached the head of the stairs, he bolted down all four flights in succession.

***

The knock took Beth by surprise and she let the books she was holding cascade onto the leather sofa. Coming out of the snug, she smiled as she recognised her visitor through the full-length glass pane of the front door.

"Gendarme Clergue, this is a surprise. How are you?"

Clergue offered his hand for her to shake. "I'm fine, Madame Samuels, and please call me Thibault."

Holding the door open wide and expecting him to walk in, she asked, "Coffee?"

"Another time, perhaps. I'm on duty and I just wanted to leave this for Jacques." He handed her a letter. "He knows where to find me if he wants to discuss the contents, and I think he will."

Turning the envelope over to see who it was from, Beth recognised the name and nodded. "I'll make sure he gets it when he comes home tonight."

Clergue smiled and replaced his cap. "It's good to see you back here again." With a broad grin on his face, he nodded and left.

As she stood in the doorway watching his progress down the short path to the gate, her last words echoed through her mind. She knew she'd responded instinctively and without thinking. *Home... Mmm I think I like that idea.* Anticipating someone coming home after work was something she hadn't been able to do for quite a while. A satisfied grin crept across her face, and she pushed the door shut.

***

Merle was the most recently completed suburb of Mende. All the detached houses were arranged in small, neatly planned clusters around the perimeter of the agreed development. The central section held a selection of low-rise apartment blocks interspersed with managed, shared gardens and tasteful planting. Only the fourth-floor apartment, or penthouse as the estate agent had referred to it, was now unoccupied in the block named *Hirondelle*.

Jacques sat on the low wall enclosing the planted raised beds and looked up at the building and then to left and right at the similar blocks that flanked it, each at a discreet distance. The fourth floor was certainly the best choice. The views from the windows at the back were unencumbered by the housing around the edge and the interior had been designed with the backdrop of the mountains as the focal point for the rooms. As Jacques had been escorted around the space, he had become more and more convinced that his search for somewhere permanent to live, now that he had had to relinquish the municipally owned house attached to the gendarmerie, was perhaps at an end. But the idea of making this address his was still not absolutely clear in his mind. Walking back to his motorbike, he folded the paperwork and put it in his pocket. He needed to talk to Beth in detail first. She knew he was looking for somewhere; they'd discussed it during their conversations online whilst she had been in England. But she didn't yet know that he had found this place. He wanted to keep it as a surprise for her return. He felt sure that if she saw the place she would love it and then perhaps he could move their relationship onto a more permanent footing.

I need to be careful not move too fast too soon.

Helmet on, he revved the engine and carefully negotiated his route around the complex and out onto the main road.

His next appointment was with an ex-employee who had been assigned to work at Vaux Consulting, and who lived on the terraces of housing stretching across Les Hautes de la Bergerie, no more than a five-minute ride away.

As he knocked on the door of the apartment, he could hear music from inside.

When the door opened, Jacques offered his card. "Jacques Forêt, Vaux Investigations, to see Nicolas Durand."

The young man stood back to let him in. "Through there, and please take a seat."

The flat was small and sparsely furnished, and its owner in his mid to late twenties, Jacques guessed.

"What is this about?" Nicolas turned off his iPod but remained standing.

"I'm conducting an internal investigation into working practices and allegations of breaches of security at Vaux Consulting, and I think that you may be able to provide me with some insight into the company during the time that you were working there."

"OK, but I wasn't with them that long, you know." Nicolas sat in the only other chair across from Jacques.

"You were employed by Vaux for what period?"

"Four and a half months. From April to August."

"And before that you worked for C and C Consulting. Is that, right?"

Nicolas nodded.

"What were your duties at Vaux?"

"I just worked on the admin team. My work varied from day to day, but was mostly photocopying, inputting information to the shared spreadsheets and project plans on the open access area of the office network. Collating papers for meetings, making coffee. Mostly everything that no-one else wanted to do."

"And did you enjoy your time there?"

"Not really."

Jacques waited, sensing there was more but Nicolas just shrugged.

"Photocopying... So you must have had sight of highly confidential documents then. For tenders, maybe... Financial documents perhaps?"

Nicolas thought for a moment. "Am I allowed to talk to you about this? I did sign a confidentiality agreement when I first joined the company, and as far as I can remember it is still valid even though I don't work for Vaux any longer."

Jacques smiled. "Yes, I know. I have a copy of it here," and he pulled out of his bag Nicolas' personal file and opened it to show him. "Just to remind you, you cannot divulge details of financial information nor details of tenders. But once the tender is settled and the work awarded, the nature of such information changes." Jacques knew he would be on difficult ground if his interviewee pressed him to be more precise. He was hoping that Nicolas was not too savvy about such matters, and that he would be able to glean some useful information that would at least point him in a direction that might be worth pursuing.

Nicolas nodded. "Yes, I sometimes did copy information for bids for work, but it was never the financial details. I wouldn't understand it anyway, even if I was given it to copy."

"And was this usual? Something you did regularly?"

Nicholas frowned. "Copying the non-confidential information happened all the time. But the confidential papers? No. I can only remember it happening twice. Mademoiselle Lapointe asked me once and the other time was for Hélène Hardi. She was in charge of the admin team."

"Can you remember which work projects the papers were for?"

"I'm really not sure I should be telling you this."

"I do have authority to go to Vaux Consulting and access

all of their files for the last 18 months if I want to. But I would rather know where to look than to just gradually work my way through the whole filing system. You'll save me a lot of time and your information could be vital, Nicolas. Anything you tell me will remain between us."

Nicolas frowned. "OK. They were both for work in Le Puy. The first one was for a two-year project to re-structure a company and retrain and re-skill staff, and the second was a refit of offices. I really can't remember any details of the money involved but I do remember that Hélène insisted that I copy the documents immediately and that she stood beside me whilst I did it and collected the originals and copies from me as soon as it was done."

"So, if it was that important, why didn't she do the copying herself?"

Nicolas let out an exasperated gasp. "You don't know what she's like to work for!"

Jacques sat back. "So, tell me about it, then."

"Hélène thinks she's running the whole organisation. She's always dropping names and talks as though the senior managers are her best friends. She thinks she is so clever. I mean, she's a smoker, you know! How clever is that when you think about what we know now about the causes of lung cancer? And she gives the impression she knows everything and everyone."

Jacques suppressed a smile.

"It was that bitch that got me fired." Nicolas' tone had hardened.

"I thought your contract was only casual and just wasn't renewed." Jacques flicked through the papers in the file and scanned the copy of the two-paragraph letter that confirmed his own statement.

"Huh! Is that what she told you? No. My contract was casual, that's true. But it was Hélène who interviewed me and it was she who said at the interview, in answer to my direct question, that an initial contract would be drawn up for six months, and that it would then be reviewed at the end of that period, so there may be the possibility of further work. I passed my probationary period, and then everything changed." He stood and moved to the window. "If you really want to know what goes on in that place," he said, spinning round to face Jacques and pointing, "then go down to the underground car park at the back of the building where the smokers congregate, and you'll find out that's where she spends most of her time. She stands there gossiping. Constantly talking about other people. And it's never complimentary."

Jacques thought for a moment. "Is this the letter you received?" He showed Nicolas the page he had in front of him.

"No. That's nothing like the letter I received." He left the room and returned a few moments later. "This is what I got," he said, thrusting a piece of paper at Jacques.

In the small meeting room on the third-floor Jacques had the letter Nicolas had given him and the one in the file side by side on the table. He noted the similarities and differences and made a note to consult HR. Swivelling round in his chair, he stared out of the window and mulled over Nicolas' assertion about the smoking area and decided it might be quite easily monitored with a discreetly angled security camera.

Sound might be a problem, but a couple of days' footage, maybe a week's, should be all that I'll need, perhaps.

A light tap on the door brought him back to his next interviewee, and he gathered Nicolas' papers together and put them face down on the floor beside his chair as Aimée walked in.

"Please sit down and I will try to take up as little as possible of your valuable time. According to your personal file, Aimée, you've been working in this field for about five years. Is that, right?"

"Yes, but I've only been working here since July last year."

"Did you know Nicolas Durand?"

Aimée smiled. "Of course, he was part of the admin

team."

"And was he a committed member of the team?"

"Yes, I think so. He always delivered whatever I asked him to on time. I rarely had to ask him to change things or do things again. I got the impression he was happy here but then he was let go."

"Were you surprised at that?

Aimée started to speak and then hesitated. "Yes, at first, but later, no."

"Why the change of opinion?"

Aimée frowned and shifted in her chair. "I really don't think I can say."

"Aimée, anything that you tell me, or anything that you know or think you know, will stay between us. It's for me to decide if it is relevant to the investigation." Jacques waited for her response. "If you don't tell me, someone else will, or I'll find out some other way. But if there is something that you think might help me then it will save a lot of time."

He watched as she chewed her bottom lip and let her gaze stray to the window.

"I didn't know he'd been sacked until he didn't come back to the office after his leave in August. We'd been… I'd been out with him a couple of times just before we both went on leave and I was looking forward to seeing him when I got back. And when I asked where he was I was told he'd been sacked."

"Sacked? Are you sure about that?"

She nodded.

"So, he wasn't on a short term casual contract, then?"

"Oh yes, he was. A six-month contract with an option to be extended. Whilst he was on leave, he got a letter telling him not to return along with his final pay."

Jacques grimaced. "I'm no expert but that seems an unfair practice to me."

"I'm told it happens all the time here." She shrugged. "But, I think you're right. It does seem an unjust thing to do."

Jacques made a note to ask the HR Director if this was

standard policy and then quickly added the initials of a couple of her senior managers with whom he could cross-check the answer. "What do you think really happened?"

"I don't... I'm not sure, Jacques. I haven't seen Nicolas since the summer. I've texted him a couple of times but he hasn't replied, so I don't know what his version of events is."

"Would you like to speculate?"

Aimée scowled, but after a few moments said flatly, "Hélène happened. She has this way of dealing with people that traps them into situations that they can't get out of and then she uses the consequences against them. I'm not saying that's what she did to Nicolas, because I don't know. But, I think that, even if she wasn't wholly responsible, if you dig deep enough, you'll find she's involved somewhere. But, I've been told you've got a desk in the operations area now, so just watch and see what happens. You were a policeman. I'm sure you'll work it out for yourself, and I suppose that you'd prefer to gather your evidence directly than second hand from me."

Jacques nodded and smiled.

wednesday, october 14th, 1.41am

"I turned over and you weren't there."

Jacques stretched out his hand towards her. "I need to tell you something."

Beth sat beside him and snuggled against his bare chest as his arm encircled her. "You're cold."

"I have a recurring dream, Beth. I never know when it will happen. Sometimes it is weeks or months before it comes back to me, and sometimes it's only a few days. And it's always at the same time. Just after one-thirty in the morning." He pulled her closer to him. "Sometimes I wake up before the end, sometimes not, and those are the worst times. That's when I wake up screaming in remembered pain." He rested his cheek against the top of her head. "I don't know if I will ever be free of it."

"Do you want to talk about it?"

"Not right now, Beth. There's a lot to tell and I still don't know if I can handle that yet."

"OK. It doesn't matter, Jacques. But I'm here whenever you're ready." She snuggled even closer.

"What are you up to today?" Jacques took the last piece of Beth's croissant from her plate.

"Hey! That's mine. And I'm taking photos in the woods today."

He stopped putting papers in his bag and looked at her.

"And that's your concerned frown, Jacques. What's the matter?"

"I don't think it's such a good idea to be in the woods. Gaston has got a hunting party here all week and I'm not sure where their stands will be."

"Don't worry. I will check that with Gaston, and I'll be careful." She walked with him to the front door.

"I'll see you tonight and we'll talk in detail about the apartment in Merle."

Beth nodded and kissed him.

***

The operations area had emptied of staff by nine that morning and at just before ten, Jacques saw Roger Baudin, coat over his arm, leave his office along with his senior manager. *Two less to worry about.* On the pretext of arranging an interview time with Édouard and Mademoiselle Lapointe, notebook in hand he strolled along the corridor to the end suite of offices. As usual, Édouard and his PA were in his office with the door closed and would be for at least the next hour, as was always the case on a Wednesday. To complete his ruse, he left a note on Mademoiselle's desk and left.

Out on the landing, he took the stairs straight down to the parking area where Serge was waiting for him, as planned.

"I can have a pinhole camera installed just there," he said, pointing up to a metal grill that was let into the wall above the housing, into which the full length roller door retracted when activated, at the rear entrance to the underground car park. "It will be fitted behind the grill, and it can be linked into the office network and the feed, including audio, will go directly to a hidden drive on the network that only you can access."

"So, if I want to view the feed, I have to be here in the office and at my desk. That's not ideal, Serge."

"Not necessarily." He stubbed out his cigarette on the side of the ashcan and pushed it into the sand in the centre. "The recordings from all the security cameras in and around both Vaux buildings are stored on the network on a daily basis and you can access them as and when you need to. Each file is automatically deleted after one month. But you

31

can also access them remotely using your secure login."

Jacques frowned. "What's that?"

"It's chilly here; let's go to my office." He activated the gate and moved across the parking area to the stairs. "The login that you have for the network here in the office can also be used from a laptop remotely. But you need an access key – a specific code – to get into the network, and the IT people can sort that out for you."

As they emerged from the stairwell into the foyer Serge fell silent and, without acknowledging his two staff on the front desk, he went straight to his office door, unlocked it and took his place behind his desk.

"Make sure the door is properly shut," he said as Jacques followed him through. "The access key will enable you to dial into the office network from any computer, but I would recommend that you use one of ours from the IT department. All the directors have them, along with most of the senior staff. Considering the nature of your work I'm surprised you weren't automatically given one on joining the company."

"I prefer the personal approach and, whilst I understand the power of the net and can handle computers, I decided when I joined that I would try not to take the work home. So yes, I was offered a laptop, but I refused."

"Well, now you will need it." He turned his own laptop round so that Jacques could see the screen. "When you log in remotely this is the screen you will see, use your access code here…" Serge keyed in his. "And then you will see the usual screen and you just log in as normal. The files from the new camera will be downloaded to a discreet drive on the network. Only you will have access to that."

"What about the IT department? Won't they also be able to access it?"

"Only you and I and the senior network administrator will know that the new drive is there and it will be set up for password access only. So, the first thing that you will need to do is to create a new and secure password. Anyone else looking at the network will not be able to see the hidden drive created for you as they can only access the parts of the network that are open to everyone or for which they have been given specific access. Ok?"

"Got it. How long will it take to do this?"

"A couple of days to install the camera, probably. Certainly, by Monday of next week everything should be in place."

It was getting dark when Jacques pulled up outside the gendarmerie in Messandrierre. Through the glass and metal door, the light spilled out as Gendarme Clergue tapped at the keyboard on his desk behind the short public counter.

"Good to see you, Jacques." The slow tapping stopped as Clergue got up.

"Thibault, you left a letter with Beth yesterday. We need to talk."

Clergue lifted the counter so that his visitor could slip through. Jacques perched on the edge of what had been his desk only a few months previously.

"As I'm sure you realise, the letter was from Juan de Silva's family and they want to—"

"They want to know if we have made any progress in his disappearance, I suppose," Clergue interrupted.

Jacques fished the letter out of his pocket. "You need to keep this and add it to the relevant file and, as ex-colleagues, can we discuss the case?"

"Of course, Jacques, but there's not much to say." Clergue resumed his place at his desk, chair pushed back into the wall behind. "Madame Pamier is still maintaining that she last saw Juan de Silva in September 2006, that he did not come with them to Messandrierre in February 2007 when they moved here permanently to look after the farm following the death of her husband's uncle. And there are no new leads." Thibault crossed his thickset arms across his chest almost in defeat.

"Frustrating. When did we last question Madame Pamier?"

Clergue pulled a file from the untidy pile in the tray on

his desk and flicked through the papers. "You last questioned her at the end of June. I went back in July to question her again and nothing since."

"Pelletier hasn't been to question her?" He frowned as Clergue shook his head in response. "That surprises me, but someone will have to take some action now that the family have made contact."

"Yes! We know, Jacques."

"Someone in this village knows something, Thibault, and it's up to you and Pelletier to find out what that is and fast."

The glower on his ex-colleague's face gave Jacques his answer. "I'll leave it with you to deal with, then."

Jacques turned and let the door slap shut behind him. By the time he had covered the few metres along the D6 to Beth's chalet, he had already developed his own plan of action.

Someone knows something, and I will find out what it is.

"Watching people when they don't know about it seems very underhand, Jacques." Beth sipped her wine.

"Yes, and I have thought about that. I've also realised that the Vaux companies may not be as well organised and managed as I've been led to believe." Jacques offered the last piece of Camembert to Beth.

"No, thanks. Why do you think that?"

"There are tensions between some of the personnel and I need to dig behind that. But I've come across something today that seems unbelievable and yet…I know what has happened is true. I have the actual evidence in my bag." He got up from the table and returned with the two letters addressed to Nicolas Durand and gave them to her. "What do you make of these?"

Beth read one after the other, and her eyes widened in disbelief. "This is either a monumental mistake made by a very inexperienced person in HR whose training needs should be addressed urgently or…" She frowned. "Or someone within your new organisation is determined to upset others. Who's done this? And why?"

"I don't know yet, but I intend to find out."

Beth frowned and scanned the letters again. "Jacques, there's information here that tells you something. Look at the references." She held the letters up and pointed to the sequences of letters and numbers at the head of each one.

Jacques took the papers from her and compared them. "Yes, I did look at that, but I couldn't make much sense of it and I'm still getting to know everyone in Édouard's half of the business."

"And is that your justification for spying on people? Do you really think that's the right way to handle this?"

Jacques shrugged. "Sometimes, no matter how distasteful, you have to take whatever opportunities are available. I don't think the evidence I can gather through the new surveillance camera will tell me everything I need to know, but it will help me to see a more rounded picture, I think. My job is to investigate the possibility of leaks of information to competitors. My experience as a policeman tells me to gather evidence, to talk to people, to observe them. I'm just doing my job, Beth."

"I know." She let out a long sigh. "So, let's leave your work at the office, shall we?"

He grinned and, taking her hand, he led her into the snug. All the papers relating to the apartment and from the estate agent were already spread out on the coffee table where Jacques had left them before dinner. "So, what do you really think?"

Beth put her glass down and picked up the plan. "It's a big place just for one, Jacques, but on paper it looks great."

"I wasn't really planning on being there all by myself all of the time."

"Yes… I think I do know that, but I was hoping… thinking…that we could keep things as they are at the moment. I'm still not sure that I can make a life out here for myself. We talked about me moving here permanently a couple of weeks ago, and I said I would think about it. And I have. But, there's a lot to consider. I've still got the remains of Dan's businesses at home, and I need to make some difficult decisions in relation to those. I still want to grow my new photography venture, not just at home but here as well, and my idea was to turn the upstairs bedroom into a studio and to use this as my base, but…Merle is the other side of Mende – that's 30 kilometres away… Unless I look at a commercial property there instead. I need to think about that and consider the implications." She looked away.

"But when we talked a couple of weeks ago, you seemed unsure about whether you would keep this place."

She stared at him for a moment. "That's true. And I'm still unsure about what I will do with this place in the long term. There is also the house in Leeds. I need to decide about that, too. I don't want to be pushed into something that I might regret later."

"What are you saying, Beth? That you've changed your mind about us? What?"

She pulled her hands through her shoulder-length hair. "No, I'm not saying that… Not exactly, but I…I need more time. More time to…to be sure."

"Of what?" He stood and strode across the room to the window. The valley was dark, the only light came from inside the chalet. He looked at the reflected room in the glass, the dancing flames from the logs in the fireplace and Beth, staring at the opposite wall, hunched forward, her face held in her hands.

"It's me, isn't it? It's me you're not sure of." Returning to her side, he squatted down beside her and took her hands in his. "That's what this is about, isn't it?"

"And myself, and moving to another county. It's a very big decision." she whispered.

He gently stroked away a stray strand of hair. "I'm not going anywhere, Beth. Whatever you decide, I will accept and I will make it work for us both. I just want you to know that and to remember it."

thursday, october 15th

"According to your personnel file, Madeleine, you've been working here since the end of 2004. Did you move from your previous job directly to this one?"

"Yes. I knew I was coming here before I left Paris, Jacques. I was head-hunted, and it wasn't the first time I'd been offered a post here, either." Madeleine's mouth creased into the beginnings of a smirk. "I know what you're thinking, Jacques."

"No, you don't, and I would like you to just answer my questions."

"You're thinking that I must have known about this job weeks, possibly months, before we stopped seeing each other, aren't you?"

Jacques tapped his pen against his notebook, but remained silent.

"But we can talk about that later, can't we?"

"No. Whilst you've been here, I presume that you've been instrumental in putting together the tenders for work throughout your tenure?"

"Yes, I've provided plans, human resource flow, some costings, in fact, the basis for most of the tenders over that time."

"Take a look at this list and let me know if you were involved in all or only some of these bids?"

She took the sheet from him and gradually read through each project name in turn.

"Yes, I was involved in all of these. But so were other senior colleagues in other parts of the company."

Jacques noticed that the hard edge was back in her voice. He retrieved the list, made a note in one corner and added his initials and the date.

"Your current project, Madeleine – what are your specific responsibilities?"

"I head up the planning and communications team. I have a total of twenty-five staff that work for me, all Vaux employees, but I also manage some client employees with relevant skills. I manage the work set out on the plan, and at the regular Stakeholder Forum I represent the team and provide input and feedback on progress. I also attend all senior internal project forums."

"That's a lot of power. Would you say that Édouard listens to you and takes on board your recommendations for tenders?"

"Of course, but he knows his own mind, Jacques. I can only inform and advise. The final decision on the content of a tender, what we tender for, is Édouard's in conjunction with his management board."

"So, it has never occurred to you, perhaps, to inflate your costings or change a plan so that a Vaux bid would be disregarded in favour of another bid from a rival firm?"

"No."

"Do you keep in touch with ex-colleagues from other companies?"

A grin crossed her face. "Yes, I do. You already know that I do, because in this business it's important to maintain a network of contacts and to stay in touch. I'm sure you've remembered that from our time together in Paris."

She can't stop herself, can she? Jacques made another note.

"Your people, Madeleine. Would you say they were a happy team?"

Her eyes bored into him. "Yes, I would, Jacques. I make a point of ensuring that my team are well looked after."

"I see. Can you tell me why your particular work area has had the most changes in personnel over the last five years in comparison with other teams?"

"I dispute that and I don't like what you're implying—"

"I'm not implying anything, Madeleine," he said, his

voice raised above hers. "I've been looking at who has worked for whom, and your work area has had the most changes of staff. It's a fact." He slid another sheet of paper across the table to her. "I'm just interested in your explanation for this?"

Madeleine stared at the spreadsheet. Every work area was detailed and for each of the five years listed her team showed the most leavers, most joiners and a staff turn-over ratio of between five and seven percent above the next nearest work area of Finance.

"This is the first time I've seen these figures, so forgive me for questioning their validity. Who has prepared this and why haven't I been informed?"

And there's that hard, grating edge in your voice again, Madeleine. Jacques was still, his attention focused on her face, pen poised to note her reaction when it came.

"Mademoiselle Lapointe put the information together at my request and I am informing you now."

"I see." She repeatedly scraped her short fine hair back behind her left ear as she stared at the sheet. "Not that she knows a great deal about how my team work but, I do employ a lot of people on short-term contracts. The admin team come within my remit and it is difficult to get decent staff, and when you do, they don't stay long because they are always looking for the next promotion."

"And the more senior staff on longer contracts? Take another look at the spreadsheet, Madeleine." Jacques waited as she scanned the columns again.

"I sometimes have to change staff around depending on their development needs and the changing remit of the work. I don't see anything unusual in that. In fact, I think that's of benefit to the work, the team as a whole and the company."

"Interesting point of view. To me, and I know I'm only an ex-policeman, Madeleine, but looking at those statistics, your results stand out from every other work area in the company. If you ignore the line that relates to your part of the organisation, the results for all the rest look on a par with each other. A slight peak here for Finance and a small dip here for IT, but overall the figures show that the company workforce is stable. Add your results in and suddenly you have a work area that is completely different. A work area with what appears to be constantly changing staff is what I would call a problem work area."

Madeleine, her face fixed, sat in stony silence.

"You have no view on that?"

Jacques watched and waited as she maintained her *froideur*. "All right. Going back to the contracts that Vaux has lost over recent months. You've supplied information on the bids for that work?"

"Yes."

"Have you taken any of the documentation out of the office or shown it to anyone outside of this company?"

"That question is insulting, Jacques!"

"You've admitted that you maintain, and keep in contact with, a network of people who work for rival companies. I have to ask the question. Now, please answer it?"

"No!"

"Is that no you won't answer the question or is that no you are not guilty of a breach of confidence?"

"No, I am not guilty of a breach of confidence."

"What about C and C Consulting? Do you know anyone there?" Jacques kept a close eye on her.

"I know the company and I have come across a few of their employees, but I wouldn't say that I know anyone there." She stared him straight in the eye.

"And what about corporate events? You say it is important in your position to maintain a network of colleagues, is that how you keep in touch?"

"Yes, mostly through events. But I also meet and catch up with people in my network at training seminars and in the course of general business on a daily basis."

"So, you will have everyone's phone number in your contacts list, for example?"

Madeleine scowled. "Where are you leading with this, Jacques?"

"I'm just establishing how closely in touch you are with your network, that's all."

She narrowed her eyes and stared at him. "Regularly. I am in contact with them regularly as my business needs dictate."

Jacques recognised the ice-cold look. She'd used it on him before. He wondered whether to risk more questions or to let her stew. Taking a different tack, he flipped his notebook shut and sat back in his chair.

"How is Xavier? I presume he left Paris with you to move here for your new job?"

"That's personal! You have no right—"

"Don't I? It was him you left me for, as I remember." His muscles bristled with tension as he watched the colour of rage creep up her neck and flood her cheeks.

She scraped her hair back and, after a moment she took a deep breath as a smile of triumph began to creep across her face. "I thought we were only talking about work and your case today, Jacques."

"We have, and now I'm finished." He stood, collected his papers and notebook and marched out of the room without a single glance back, and his pace did not slow until he had reached the entrance to his own building.

The village of Messandrierre was eerily quiet that evening. The bar had only two customers from the hunting party with Marianne to tend to their drinks. No light escaped from around or through the slats of the shuttered windows of the houses, except for the Mancelle property where Marie was at home with her son, Pierre, who was suffering from a nasty chest infection. By contrast, the windows of the meeting room on the first floor of the *Mairie* were alive with a fogged yellow light as Monsieur le Maire – Monsieur Mancelle senior – conducted one of his regular municipality meetings.

"*Mesdames et Messieurs.* You've had time to think about the consequences of the plans for strengthening and re-surfacing the main road and how it might affect you. Can I

41

ask for your comments, please?"

Fermier Rouselle was on his feet in an instant. "Monsieur Mancelle, the closure of the cattle tunnel under the *route nationale* to help strengthen the road at that point will not affect me that much. I have pastures to the north of the village as well as the south, and I can transport and graze my animals wherever I like. But there are some in this village whose livelihoods will be put at serious risk if this plan goes ahead. Fermier Delacroix and Madame Pamier are just two examples. There are others. I object to this plan in the strongest possible terms, Monsieur." He sat down to a round of applause, murmurs of support and a studiously puzzled look from Delacroix.

The *Maire* stood and raised his hands to quell the noise. "Madame Pamier, your thoughts, please."

"This plan will affect my business greatly, Monsieur le Maire. I only have pastures on the southern side of the village, and I would have to hire transport for my beasts if I could not herd them through the tunnel under the road. I can not in all conscience consider moving them across the road because of the traffic. It would be too dangerous, Monsieur, and that is why the tunnel was created for us some years ago, but…" A ripple of light applause interrupted her and she paused to let it subside. "But there is another point that I want to raise: remembrance. My husband's family has been in this village for generations. Their graves are in the village cemetery on the other side of the N88. Under this new plan, how will I be able to visit the graves in remembrance, Monsieur? More importantly, when we have a funeral, how will we pay our respects if we have no access to the graveyard?"

The murmur that had started in one corner of the room as Madame Pamier sat down to await a response, rose to a crescendo, a mixture of aggrieved comments directed at the *Maire* and raised voices in support for Madame.

"Please…*Mesdames et Messieurs*…please let me respond?" The *Maire* waited for the noise to subdue to a level that he could talk over. "Madame Pamier, thank you for your contribution, and I acknowledge your concerns. I know how important family is to you and your husband. I regularly see you as you walk through the village taking flowers to the graves of your loved ones. I understand why you do so, and I realise that keeping the tunnel open would be safer. But surely, just a little care and attention when crossing the N88 would be sufficient to keep you safe in future."

Madame Pamier stood immediately. "You say that now, Monsieur, but what about in twenty or thirty years' time when my hearing is not so good and my eyes are starting to fail. Will it be safe for me then to visit the family graves? Will it?"

The room erupted with cries of '*Non!*' and '*Impossible!*', and Fermier Rouselle stood again to make a further point. "Monsieur Mancelle, I agree with Madame Pamier. The proposal means that we would be cut off from our own graveyard as well as our southern pastures. I tell you again that we must oppose this idea in the strongest possible terms. I also demand that you answer Madame's question in relation to how we would bury one of our own if we could not access the graveyard?" Rouselle, his cheeks flushed and a hard stare, sat down and let the other villagers barrack their elected representative.

"*Mesdames et Messieurs...*" His arms outstretched in supplication, the *Maire* tried again to bring the meeting back to order. "*Mesdames et Messieurs*, please allow me to answer," he shouted.

The barracking continued until Rouselle stood again and held up his hands. Gradually, the raised voices subsided to a belligerent murmur.

Jacques, sitting at the back of the room, exchanged a concerned look with Gendarme Clergue.

"Thank you, *Mesdames et Messieurs*. It has been suggested that, in place of the usual procession through the village to the cemetery, vehicles could be used to transport mourners to…"

His last words were drowned in a cacophony of cries of

'*Non!*' and '*Jamais!*' from the villagers. Fermier Rouselle stood and waited. After about 3 or 4 minutes, the voices had dissipated to a strained silence.

"I know we stood against each other in municipal elections a few months ago, Monsieur Mancelle, but you won the final vote by a margin, and I respect the choice made by my fellow villagers. I also accept that you are a gifted businessman who has done a lot for this community. So, I say what I say next as a statement of fact and not as an insult. I have no wish to cause offence. We are a small, close-knit community, Monsieur. You were not born in the village nor was your father, and it was your grand-father who chose to leave his ailing parents and younger brother with your family farm to manage. You are an in-comer. You do not fully understand our traditions and our ways, or if you ever did, you have forgotten anything you might have been taught. We have carried our loved ones through the village to the graveyard on foot for generations. That is how we honour our dead, Monsieur. That is how we have always done this. Where do you think that we are going to find the money for vehicles to transport mourners the 450 metres to our graveyard. It is a preposterous suggestion! Have you forgotten the tragedy that led to the cattle tunnel being built? Do you even know why it was built?"

Rouselle paused momentarily for an answer, but none came. "I thought so! Like you, Monsieur, the *Consul Général's* office, the *Préfecture*, all those in control, have forgotten. You and they do not understand us or our ways. We have always carried our dead to the cemetery ourselves. It is our right to do that. A right established over decades. It is our right to have safe access to our graveyard." Rouselle underlined his last three sentences with a forceful pointed thrust of his outstretched right arm.

The occupants of the room stood as one being and applauded as Jacques leaned across to Clergue. "There is a solution, you know, Thibault, but I think it needs to come from you."

Clergue nodded. "But I would need some assistance and

do you think Fournier would agree?"

"It's a municipal matter, Thibault. What Fournier doesn't know about, he can't complain about, and let Mancelle fight it out with him. He's the *Maire*, not you, and I can always step in and help if you need me to."

Clergue remained standing as people began to take their seats and a tense silence returned to the room. "I think we have a solution that can meet all needs, Monsieur le Maire. Perhaps we can discuss it in detail outside of the meeting."

"Thank you, Gendarme Clergue, and we will talk in the morning." The *Maire* consulted his agenda and returned to his own chair behind the table set in front of the gathered crowd. "I think the next item is in relation to the campsite. Gaston, the floor is yours."

Gaston stood. "Monsieur le Maire, thank you. As you know I've been concerned about the potential loss of income from the campsite as a result of free camping. In July and August, I, Gendarme Clergue and ex-Gendarme Forêt worked shifts to enable us to catch as many people as possible who were taking advantage of the facilities provided without paying. Over those two months we collected 23% more revenue as a result. In other months of the year, any potential loss of income would probably be a lot less. I think that the municipality must look at how we can make the campsite more secure to ensure that we can capture at least some of this lost revenue."

The *Maire* remained seated and smiled broadly. "Thank you, Gaston. First of all, I want to formally thank you, Gendarme Clergue and Monsieur Forêt for the work that you put in over the summer. I understand that my grandson, Junior Gendarme Mancelle, helped with this, so we must record our thanks to him also."

The room applauded as Beth, a grin on her face, whispered in Jacques' ear, "That's child exploitation! He's only five years old, Jacques. You should be ashamed of yourself!"

He took her hand and squeezed it. "He's six now, and he'll make an excellent policeman, one day."

"How is Pierre, Monsieur?" It was Madame Rouselle who asked. "I know he hasn't been at school this last week."

"He's at home tucked up in bed, but he will be well enough to go to school in a few days or so. Thank you for your concern. Back to business, we will consider your proposal in council." He referred to his agenda and then addressed the floor. "Before I bring the meeting to a close, are there any remaining questions or issues that anyone would like to raise?"

Gaston stood for a second time. "Monsieur le Maire, since the restaurant in Montbel closed in July, I have been gradually picking up more and more of their business and that is a good thing, both for me and the rest of the village. However, it does mean that I have less time to spend on my other duties within the municipality. I think that being responsible for the Salle des Fêtes, the bar and the restaurant should now become my sole remit, and I was wondering if we could find another way of managing the campsite."

Gaston's question brought a reluctant and taut silence to the meeting, and the *Maire* thought for a moment before responding.

"Yes," he said and paused. "Yes, I can see why you think that relinquishing your duties in relation to the campsite might be a solution. We will discuss it in council, Gaston, and thank you for bringing this to my attention." Standing, he looked across his audience and smiled. "If that is all, I will close the meeting. Let's go over to the bar and relax with a drink. Gaston, charge the first round to me, please."

The room emptied into the chill night air and Jacques and Beth, hand in hand, strolled a few steps behind the rest of the village.

"What was the terrible tragedy that Fermier Rouselle talked about?"

"Some time in the seventies, a truck carrying newly felled trees, heading for the sawmill between here and Mende, came down from the *col* too fast. It was mid-

46

September, it was raining and the driver lost control of his vehicle. It jack-knifed and ploughed into the herd that one of Rouselle's uncles was driving across the road. I'm not sure of all of the details, but I think the truck driver was killed. Rouselle lost his uncle and one of the farmhands, another farmhand was injured and the herd scattered, and as a result some had to be put down and two were killed outright by the impact."

Beth looked across Jacques to the road. It was silent and, under the dark cloudy sky, almost imperceptible against the black of the mountains beyond. "Madame Pamier was right. Even now, visibility isn't that good, is it?"

"Not really. But you don't need to worry about that. I'm certain Thibault and Monsieur le Maire can work something out and if necessary I'll step in and help too."

"But I do need to worry about what happens here, Jacques, if I'm going to be spending a lot of time here." She released his hand and slipped hers around his arm.

He smiled at her. "Do you want to go the bar with everyone else or just go back to the chalet?"

"The chalet."

"Ok. Now I've got you all to myself it gives me a chance to ask you how your visit to see Old Thierry went?"

"It was acutely embarrassing, Jacques."

He turned towards her and stopped. "How so?"

"He wants me to take all his photographic equipment. Which is fine in principle, and I was very flattered that he thought I might be interested. But when I asked him how much he wanted for it, he refused to say."

Jacques smiled. "That's Old Thierry! He is the most-mild mannered, gentlemanly and generous man I know. His offer would have been genuine and rather than expecting to give you a price he would have been hoping that you would make an offer."

"I see! I wish I'd known that sooner."

"Do you want to take him up on his offer?"

Beth let out a long sigh. "It would be really nice to do that, but he has some lenses that are worth, easily between

€350 and €500. He also has some cameras that a collector could only dream about, which was why I had to refuse his offer. It was far, far too generous, Jacques. I couldn't, in all conscience, accept."

"Beth, whilst you were in England, Thierry never stopped talking about your photographs from the Fête St Jean in June. He was also very impressed with your artistry on the portraits that you did of the other villagers. As was Madame Rouselle. She has become your ambassador here."

"I see." Beth remained silent as they skirted the bar and took the road up towards Rieutort. Head bowed she watched her feet as they traversed the tarmac for a few steps. "The work on the portraits… It's not that difficult. You've seen the software I use. It's just manipulation of the photo, that's all. Anyone can do it."

"But Thierry can't. You have to remember that he will be ninety soon and he has not been well for some time. He recognises that, with digital photography, the world has changed so much and so rapidly that it has become alien to him. That's why he sees you as his successor."

Beth took the key from her pocket and let them in. "Mmm, he gave me the names and addresses of three couples who wanted to book him for their wedding photographs. One couple is getting married next month and the other two next year. Apparently, he has shown them my work and they are happy that I undertake the commission." She kicked off her shoes, left them by the door and threw her coat over the banister of the spiral staircase as she passed. "I haven't contacted any of the couples yet. I wasn't really sure if I should. It feels a bit like I'm stealing his livelihood."

Jacques followed her into the snug and took her in his arms. "It's not stealing, Beth. It's an opportunity. Thierry has given you this work because he knows you are the best person for the job."

She frowned. "I know, but I've only done a few weddings, just for family and a couple of friends. I'm concerned that I might not be able to match up to his well-established and well-known standards, and other people's long-held expectations."

"So, that's what this is all about!" He hugged her closer. "You're far too talented to fail, Beth. Just believe in yourself for once."

friday, october 16th

"Will you meet me for lunch today?"

Beth nodded.

"Good, afterwards we can go to Merle and look at the apartment…if you're interested?" Jacques packed his papers into his bag.

"Of course, I'm interested. It's going to be your place and probably your permanent space. I want to see it and to share your hopes and thoughts for it…"

"But you're not sure you want to share it with me, right?"

"I just need more time, that's all. I don't really know if I can make a life here, yet. I need to convince myself." She smiled up at him. "Where are we meeting and what time?"

"OK. Half past twelve at the Drap d'Or, then."

"Jacques, really nice to meet you after all this time. I've heard so much about you from Madeleine." Hélène Hardi shook his hand firmly, a bright smile on her face, and then sat opposite him. "I was so sorry to hear that you and Madeleine had split up—"

"I'm sure your time is precious, Hélène, and I don't want to keep you from your work any longer than is necessary." Consulting her personal file, he glanced at the papers, looked up at her, smiled and said, "I see you've worked here since January 2005."

Hélène nodded.

"And that you've worked with Madeleine since arriving here. Is that correct?"

She nodded again. Jacques continued to stare at the papers on the table as he wondered exactly what it was that she knew about his previous relationship with Madeleine.

Looking through her application to join Vaux Consulting, he turned to the section that detailed her work experience.

"You've worked in Paris, too, and I've noticed that you were employed there before you came to Mende, and before that you were working in Rouen and prior to that, it was Orléans." *All of which mirrors Madeleine's career path.* Looking up, he grinned. "That's quite a bit of the country that you've covered, Hélène."

"It is. I'm lucky enough to be free to be able to please myself." She let out a girlish giggle and shrugged.

Grow up! His face remained composed as he addressed his next question to her and watched for her response. "I notice that you resigned from each of those previous posts. Would you like to tell me why?"

She shifted slightly in her chair and then smiled. "I went on to a better paid job with more responsibility. I see project management as my career path now and I intend—"

"So, it was nothing to do with following Madeleine from job to job." Before she could answer, he continued, "Nothing to do with Madeleine finding those jobs for you and recruiting you herself?"

"I just want to say—"

"As she did for your post here, I suggest."

Slapping the flat of her hand on the table, Hélène sat upright, her round cheeks flushed, her voice raised. "I just want to say—"

"I've checked with your last employer, Hélène. You were under investigation for intimidation of a junior employee at the time you left. Would you like to tell me about that?"

She pushed her glasses up to the top of her nose. "It's none of your business," she spat. "Your remit is to undertake an internal investigation for this company. What happened before I came here is of no concern of yours."

"I'll be the judge of that." He stared at her across the table until she finally looked away.

"Can you take a look at this list, please, and tell me if you've provided any information for any of these tenders for work."

Hélène worked her way through the list assigning ticks as she scanned the page. "Just those I've noted," she said as she tossed the page down in front of Jacques.

"What sort of information did you provide?"

"Mostly details of the human resource flow for an admin team, some costings for materials and base tasks for the project plan, but that's all."

"Did you show details to anyone outside the company?"

"Of course not!" She frowned.

"But, like Madeleine, I suppose you keep in touch with a network of people in other companies who have the same field of expertise as you, is that right?"

Hélène's face brightened. "Naturally. How else can I keep moving from post to post and keep improving my prospects? It's also really important to keep on top of the latest information about current business practices, what's new that's coming up and what's old that's—"

"You're openly admitting that you discuss your work with people outside the company, is that right?"

"No. But I do like to debate—"

"So, you do talk about company business with non-company employees."

"Look, Jacques, I discuss business policies and practices, that's all."

He noticed the grating sound in her voice and decided to push her further. "Have you discussed the policies within this company that relate to costing up tenders for work?"

"No. Well, perhaps, but—"

"Who with?"

"There's no need to shout."

"I'm not. Just answer the question."

Hélène squirmed. "I may have mentioned to people in the smoking area that we sometimes build in a narrow margin on our costings."

"Who?"

"I can't remember who and it would have just been as part of a general discussion."

Jacques contained a sigh of frustration, noted the details

and flipped his notebook shut.

"If we're finished I'll get back to—"

"We're not. I want to move on to something else." Jacques put in front of Hélène the letter that Nicolas Durand had received, terminating his employment, alongside the letter that had been in his personal file which stated that his contract was not being renewed. "What can you tell me about these two documents?"

"Nothing. I've not seen these before." Hélène looked up and smiled.

"But you do you know Nicolas Durand, don't you?"

"He worked for me for a while, but I wouldn't say that I know him." She sat back and crossed her arms.

Jacques picked up a second file of papers, sifted through them and, resting the file against the edge of the table so that she couldn't see the contents, continued. "According to the records I have here, you interviewed him, you signed the letter offering him a post, you were his designated line manager in his contract of employment, you completed his probationary report, you signed his letter acknowledging he had passed his probationary period, you completed two subsequent reports, both lengthy and detailed, about issues you discussed with him and it was to you that Personnel sent the final letter not renewing his contract for signature. I would say that you knew Monsieur Durand."

"Well, I didn't understand that was what you meant."

"I spent some time with the HR Director, one of her managers, and Mademoiselle Lapointe yesterday, Hélène, and they explained to me how personnel services operate within these two companies. So, looking at these letters and these references here, I know that this letter was drafted by one of the Personnel staff who then passed it to her manager for approval, JS, who then emailed it to Mademoiselle Lapointe, EML, who then emailed it to you to sign and issue, HH." Jacques paused to check her reaction, but she shook her head, her face expressionless.

"No. I've never seen this before."

"Mademoiselle Lapointe's record keeping is exemplary,

Hélène." He consulted his notes. "That letter was emailed to your inbox at 15.32 on Monday, July 20th because Nicolas was going on leave with effect from Monday July 27th. As far as HR and Mademoiselle Lapointe were concerned, it was important to let him know, before he took leave, that his contract would not be renewed."

Hélène shook her head. "I don't remember that."

"Let's look at the second, but very different letter." He placed it over the first letter so that the references on both were next to each other. "These sets of initials tell me that this second letter took exactly the same route from HR to you. HH are your initials, aren't they?"

"I've never seen this before."

"That's what HR and Mademoiselle Lapointe said, too. But look at the date, Hélène. It's July 20th."

"As I said, I've never seen it before. I get a hundred emails a day, maybe more. I can't remember all of them."

"But it seems that you can be quite definite about not having seen these letters."

Her face was still but her defiance was plain to see in her eyes. Jacques wondered how difficult it might be to follow the electronic trail. He decided he would seek out and talk to someone in IT.

"OK. What about the signature on that second letter? Look at it closely please and tell me if you recognise it?"

"I can't be sure, but I think that might be Aimée's initials on behalf of the HR Director." She looked up at Jacques and smiled.

And I'm expected to believe that, am I?

He picked up the evidence, collected the various files together and stood. "Thank you, Hélène. If I need to talk to you again, I will email you to arrange a convenient time and day." He strode out of the room and left the door open wide for Hélène to follow or not as she chose. He wasn't going to wait for her. As he walked through the operations area, he noticed that Aimée was not at her desk. He pulled out his phone and as he reached the landing he stopped and sent her a text.

Call me asap, please. Need to talk. Jacques Forêt

"…and you're absolutely certain you have not seen that letter nor signed it?"

Aimée cast her eyes over the document again. "I'm sure, Jacques, one hundred percent sure." She pushed it back across the table to him. "I would never change a letter that HR had drafted unless I could see a misspelling or a misuse of grammar or something of that nature. As for these extra paragraphs, I would never add in such details unless it was specifically requested. These detailed comments about inability to communicate effectively and quoting a specific example… That is wholly inappropriate. I would never do that. It's the sort of thing that should only be discussed in private as part of the performance review process. The only situation when that kind of information might be useful is when a prospective employer is asking for a reference from me about a past employee, and even then, I would not include the details of specific examples. I would just say that I'd identified areas of concern or that I'd spoken to the individual about weaknesses in his ability to communicate effectively, for example. Then I would make a comment about improvements identified or not, as required. That's about as specific as I would get. And no, that is not my annotation at the bottom of the letter on behalf of HR."

Jacques thought for a moment. "All right, and thanks for that detailed response. One last thing, then. Can I ask you for a sample of your handwriting? A simple sentence and a signature is all I require."

As Aimée swiftly copied out the first short paragraph of the letter under discussion, Jacques wondered about the electronic route of the letter. Aimée signed the sheet and passed it to Jacques. When Aimée had left the room, he compared the writing with the initials on the letter that Nicolas had actually received and nodded, then he picked up his phone and rang Philippe Chauvin.

***

Having unlocked the door, the estate agent took a step back and nodded to Jacques. Beth walked in first followed by Jacques whilst the agent remained on the landing. The octagonal vestibule was large and one of the doors hid a small cloakroom. Beth stood in the centre and slowly turned around, letting her photographer's eye take in the space. Finally, she looked up as her attention was drawn to the domed glass ceiling above, the only source of natural light.

"This space needs up-lighters. Probably one on every other wall," she said, her face impassive as she waited for Jacques to take the lead.

Jacques smiled and opened the door to the main living space. Before he had time to say anything, she had walked into the middle of the large room. Floor to ceiling retractable windows on two sides looked out onto hills and over the houses around the edge of the development below. Beth let her gaze sweep over the emptiness. Moving close to the back wall, she strolled along the perimeter of the space, breathing in the newness, taking in every centimetre, every shadow, every particle of dust that had accumulated during the relatively short time since the workmen had vacated the apartment.

"What an amazing space! There's so much you could do with this. This wall can take a single large piece of art or a photograph or a series of smaller pictures. And a sweeping balcony along two sides! This is fabulous, Jacques."

Beth turned and went to the corner of the room where the two windowed walls met. "This space here would be perfect for the dining area, I think, with patio chairs and a table outside, too."

She moved again into the kitchen area and started looking in cupboards and drawers. "Wow!"

As she stood looking into a large double pantry cupboard, she felt Jacques put his arms around her waist.

"I knew you would like it," he whispered into her ear. "The bedrooms and bathroom are this way." Taking her by the hand, he led her back out into the vestibule. Opening a door on his left, he stood back to let her enter the master bedroom. A weak sun was streaming through the windows, bathing the room in a soft, ivory light. Again, she walked the perimeter of the space. By the windows, she asked, "Will these open, and can we go out onto the balcony?"

"I'll get the agent," said Jacques as he disappeared out of the room. Beth moved closer to the windows to take in the view. The agent, followed by Jacques, unlocked and opened the one nearest to him and then left them alone. Beth stepped out into the sharp chill of the air. She leaned against the steel railings and looked back into the room.

"Blue," she said. "If I were going to choose a colour for the walls in this room, I think it would be blue. The same pale blue that the sky is today, with a mirror on that wall to reflect the light and to bring the external scenery into the room."

"Does this mean you like it?"

"Yes. I do. It's a wonderful space. There's so much you could do with it." As she walked towards him, her arms outstretched, she saw what she thought was a flicker of disappointment on his face. As she hugged him, it turned to smile. "I mean, there's a lot that *we* could do…"

***

"…that's not good enough, Jacques," Alain Vaux shouted as he walked back behind his desk. "I want to see results." He threw down a copy of an email for Jacques to read. "That article is going to appear in tomorrow morning's paper. I need to be able to say publicly that the cyber-attack was not as the result of internal action or leaks of information."

Jacques carefully replaced the pages in front of Alain and took a deep breath. "These accounts that have been copied or hacked or accessed… Do we know how many?"

"About 100,000, and that represents just under a third of that particular pension payroll that our HR directorate administers and has administered for the last four years. We cannot afford to lose that contract. That's why I need results, Jacques."

Jacques, hands behind his back, spoke calmly. "It's not that simple, and I can't guarantee that I can give the assurances you want."

"Why not?" Alain thumped his fist into the nearby wall.

"Because any current company employee can arrange for anyone – a hacker, a master criminal – to legitimately visit either of these buildings for the day, and if they have with them a memory stick, are IT-skilled and given time and access to one of the computers on the network, they can just about copy any damn thing they want."

Alain glared and lent across the desk. "What the hell does that mean?"

Jacques matched Alain's stance. "Exactly what I've just said, Alain. I've checked the list of company employees involved in each of the bids lost, along with day visitors and then matched that to the records of who has had system access. There are a number of visitors, visitors who have had authorised access to these buildings by company employees, who have also had system access, Alain. On my arrival, I advised both you and the board of my concerns about internal security, but you decided not to act."

Breaking the tension, Alain scraped his fingers across his forehead and let out a sigh and, hands in his trouser pockets, he walked over to the windows. "Which probably means there is someone within the company, who has uninterrupted access, who might be behind this."

Jacques relaxed and drew up a chair. "I'm sorry to tell you that I no longer think this investigation is just about lost contracts, Alain. Over the last week, I've come across other internal matters that lead me to believe that your whole organisation is not as tightly managed as you and your brother think. I'm not yet ready to present detailed findings, but I think that Édouard has internal management issues that need addressing. I have some concerns about the stability of the central project management team and I need to delve deeper. As for links to, and with, C and C Consulting, there are many. I still need to talk to Édouard and the Finance and

IT directors. I cannot say yet who may have leaked information – if that is what has been happening."

Alain thought for a moment. "When will you be able to present your findings, even if they are only initial thoughts?"

"Tuesday morning, at the latest, I expect."

Alain frowned his disappointment but remained silent for a moment. "And will this new surveillance camera you've had set up help you to come to a fuller conclusion sooner?"

"Who told you about that?" Jacques clenched his jaw as he waited for an answer.

"I authorised the expenditure."

saturday, october 17th

In Messandrierre, Guy Delacroix hadn't wanted to get up at such an early hour. But a job transporting cattle to the abattoir was a job, and the fact that he was doing it for Fermier Rouselle made it all the sweeter. A chill wind whistled through the barn as he stood looking at his four motors. All of them were haphazardly stood where they had been stopped when last used and most of them had not been used for the last three months. Two had bald tyres and the third had a back light out and brakes that needed adjusting. All things that he'd been meaning to get around to. But then there had not been much point as the requests to take cattle to the abattoir in Langogne from the other farmers in the area had stopped during the summer. That is, until Rouselle called to ask for his help the day before.

As he looked from one vehicle to the other, his still-fogged brain struggled to calculate the possible combined weight of the open trailer plus two of Rouselle's Aubrac cattle balanced against the recommended tow-weight for his only street-legal vehicle, the white Lada. The previous night's drinking session with his life-long friend, Douffre, had taken its toll. He attempted to frown away his hang-over as he marshalled his wits to cope with the maths, but failed on both counts.

Deciding to take the risk, he reversed the Lada up to the trailer. As he bent to fix the coupling to the tow-bar, his head began to swim and fine beads of sweat began to dot his forehead. He grabbed hold of one of the flat metal bars half way up the side of the trailer and pulled himself upright. It took a moment or two before he felt steady on his feet. He wiped the sleeve of his blue overalls across his brow. His eyesight still bleary, he only glanced at the coupling to assure himself it was secure.

Settled behind the wheel he started the engine and didn't bother with his seat belt. He was only going down the track to Ferme Rouselle and he reasoned that, for such a short distance, it didn't matter, and Gendarme Clergue was unlikely to be patrolling around the village this early. He moved the vehicle off his property onto the top road and trundled in second towards the *chateau*. Just as he reached Ferme Sithrez – now empty with the windows boarded up and the remains of the police tape flapping in the breeze – he turned right down the steep path and then right again onto the narrow track towards Ferme Pamier and the bottom road that dissected the village. The track was muddy and slippery from the overnight rain, and Delacroix almost lost control of the vehicle. He brushed his sweaty right hand down his thigh and then shifted into first and turned onto the track to Ferme Rouselle.

"You're late," barked Fermier Rouselle as Delacroix pulled up at the gate to the holding pen. "You were supposed to be here one half hour ago."

"I'm here now, aren't I?" Delacroix's tone held its usual venom.

Rouselle marched over to the pen and unlatched the large wooden gate and anchored it in position. He then moved a section of free-standing fencing and placed it opposite the open gate to create a path for the cattle that led directly to the trailer.

"Open it, then." He shot Delacroix an annoyed and pointed look.

"The money first." Delacroix rubbed his chest and frowned at the stabbing pain but did not change his stance.

Rouselle pulled out an envelope and handed it across to his neighbour. "Now, get that trailer open and let's get these beasts loaded."

A few minutes later, the beasts were secured in the trailer, the farmer strode back to his barn, Delacroix started the engine and turned the Lada in a wide arc to leave the way he had come. He was about to reach for the seatbelt when a sudden pain hit him in the centre of his chest and radiated down his left arm. He braked hard. The cattle lowed their complaints. Another pain lunged at him, but Delacroix ignored it and shifted into first and set off again. This time he made it to the track. With the trailer moving unsteadily over the uneven and soggy ground, he progressed up the incline to the top road and turned left. Accelerating on the wet and slippery tarmac, the trailer began to sway as he rounded the bend where the road forked to Rieutort. He progressed down the slope and passed the chalets, the trailer swaying with increasing force. Delacroix tried to compensate and put his foot down hard on the brake as he felt another pain slam into his chest. He keeled over the steering wheel and blacked out.

***

The slide show of photos that Beth had partially put together for her website was scrolling round and round in a loop on her laptop. The two-thirds full cup of coffee on her left had been untouched for so long, it was tepid. Her chin resting on her left hand, her right hand covering her mouse, unmoving, she had remained silent and motionless for almost half an hour. Sitting at her desk and staring out of the glass fronted loft area, her mind had been consumed by one complex thought.

How do I know I've got it right this time?

She blinked as another equally troubling thought came into her mind and diverted her attention to the future and a possible settled and permanent life in France. We need to talk, she decided, and then revised her newly made commitment.

I just need to tell him.

It was the loud grating sound and the heavily revved and uneven noise of a vehicle's engine that shocked Beth into noticing the world beyond her computer and outside her head. She ran to the window as Delacroix's vehicle veered off the road and into the ditch, the trailer sliding down after it, turning on its side and slewing along the ground until it hit a nearby tree. Almost in a daze she ran back to the desk and picked up her mobile and dialled 112. As the call connected, she sprinted down the stairs and out of the chalet, leaving the door wide open. Answering the emergency operator's questions, she ran down the slope to the scene of the accident.

The noise had brought Gendarme Clergue out of his office and when he reached the scene he moved quickly to the driver's window, reached through and pressed his fingers against Delacroix's neck and frowned.

"How long for the ambulance?" Clergue ran around to the trailer, where the cattle were on their sides one on top of the other, limbs askew, and he checked one of the tags. "Rouselle's," he said to Beth as he immediately began to dial the number for the farm. Permission given to end the beasts' suffering, Clergue took out his gun and looked at Beth who turned away and covered her ears. The two shots that rang out to silence the piercing screams of the injured cattle were partially drowned out by the siren as the emergency services turned off the RN88 and into the village.

**

The paperwork for the apartment in Merle all signed, Jacques had a broad grin on his face as he strolled across Mende to where he had parked Beth's car. Cradled in his right arm was a bottle of champagne, and his next port of call was to be his favourite charcuterie for some wild boar in Armagnac, a taste he had acquired since moving to the Cévennes.

The traffic was slow and tedious as the final vestiges of the rush hour at the end of the day drew to a close. Out on the RN88, heading north to the village, Jacques powered the car through the sharp bends along the mountainside. He stopped off in Badaroux to pick up some fresh bread and ten minutes later was taking the turn for the village. At the sight of the police tape and Gendarme Clergue in the road he pulled over.

"Thibault, what's happened here?" He let the car's engine idle.

"It's Delacroix. He lost control of his vehicle. It's not clear if he will survive. When I arrived, his pulse was erratic and weak, and the paramedics had to re-start his heart here at the road-side." Gendarme Clergue folded his arms across his chest, looked at his ex-colleague and shook his head. "He reeked of last night's whisky, Jacques. It's good that no-one else was involved."

Jacques frowned. "But it's still a waste of a life if he doesn't make it."

Thibault nodded and moved onto the grass verge to let a delivery van move past the obstruction.

"Beth saw some of what happened, and I've taken a statement from her."

"Is she all right?"

"I think so. But I had to kill the cattle Delacroix was transporting, and she was still at the scene of the accident. I think she was a bit shaken."

"Yes, that would have upset her. What about Delacroix's next of kin?"

"According to Madame Rouselle, there are some relatives in Canada, but his wife's dead and there are no children, so there's no-one here in France."

Jacques nodded and shifted into first when Thibault put a hand on the open window frame.

"Are you insured to drive that vehicle, Jacques? I only ask because someone in the village will be asking me and I want to be able to answer truthfully."

Grinning, he released the handbrake. "Naturally, don't worry, Thibault," he lied. Closing the window, he drove the final few metres to Beth's chalet.

toussaint – all saints' day,
sunday, november 1st, 11.00am

Jacques drained his coffee and returned his attention to the photos of the interior of Aimée Moreau's apartment that Pelletier had spread out on his desk.

"There doesn't seem to be much here," he said as he quickly scanned them all again. "It's almost as though something's missing, but I can't see what."

The outer office door clicked shut as Beth arrived, as previously arranged. With a nod between the two men, Jacques beckoned her into Pelletier's office.

"Beth, come in. I think you can help Magistrate Pelletier with his current investigation." Jacques took her camera bag from her and stood aside so that she had full view of the display on the desk. "These are crime scene photographs, taken yesterday after the body had been removed. I just want you to look at them and tell me what you see?"

She flicked through the first few. "Good photographs. Sharp."

"It's not the quality of the photographs that I'm interested in, Madame Samuels. I'm just interested in what you can see in them."

Beth nodded and then began setting the photos out in rows, grouping them so the shots from each room were all together. She studied the arrangement carefully.

"It looks a nice place. The decor is light and the furniture is very modern and functional. New almost. But it's not lived-in, is it?"

Pelletier glanced at Jacques but his face remained expressionless. "What do you mean by that?"

"Look at these of the bathroom shelves, for instance."

She bent over and scrutinised the shots again. "Everything is exactly where it should be. Two bottles of perfume in the boxes they were bought in. Mine are all in a drawer, and I always get rid of the boxes as soon as I begin to use the perfume." She stood upright and addressed Jacques. "No-one has only two perfumes that they wear. I've brought four with me, and I've got another three in my dressing table at home. You need at least two perfumes just for work. Then you need something for evening and maybe something very light for casual daytime. No self-respecting woman would have less than four or five perfumes that she wore regularly."

Jacques frowned. "OK. What else do you see?"

"Those particular perfumes are quite expensive. The one on the left would cost about £75 at home, so that's, what, about €85, almost €90? The second one would cost about twenty percent more. So, whoever she is, she must have a reasonable disposable income. And my bathroom only ever looks that tidy after I've cleaned it!"

Beth looked at the pictures again, a deep frown on her forehead. She looked up as realisation came to her. "And where's her make-up? Where's all the other stuff you need in a bathroom. All I can see is one bottle of shower gel, where's her conditioner and shampoo?"

She collected those few photos together and handed them back to Jacques.

"Tell me what you make of the bedroom?"

Beth moved them so that the photographs were separated from the rest and carefully examined each one. "This looks… I don't know. It looks like a set piece to me. Like one of those modern art installations. Except it doesn't make sense."

Jacques stood back. "That was my first thought too. The duvet is pulled back at the right-hand side of the bed but the phone is on the left bedside cabinet."

"I agree. But look at the pictures of the open wardrobe. Everything in there is perfectly arranged and colour co-ordinated. But there's only one pair of jeans and two casual shirts. All the rest is what I would use for work. It's almost as though she lives somewhere else but is spending some time in this place and has just enough to get her through the week for whatever she has to do here."

"That echoes my own thoughts. So, we need to look for another address, possibly," said Pelletier as he removed his spectacles and began to examine them for any possible smears or specs of dust.

Beth moved on to the remaining photos of the combined lounge and kitchen diner. "There are no pictures on any of the walls, which seems strange to me. I've got two pictures in the main living space at the chalet with another in the master bedroom. There isn't a single picture anywhere in this place. I don't think she lives here, well, not permanently, in my opinion."

"Anything else, Beth?"

She picked up the shots of the kitchen area. "These two empty wine glasses by the sink with the empty bottles beside them. That looks more like a still life painting than just being the result of someone putting bottles and glasses on a draining-board ready to be washed in the morning."

Pelletier frowned. "I don't understand," he said.

"Look at the juxta-positioning of the objects. The bottles set slightly apart at the back, one glass further forward but slightly to the left with the second glass laid on its side with the bowl apparently pointing to something out of the picture." She gazed at the photo. "If I didn't know that was a crime scene photo I would guess that someone had arranged those objects and then photographed them for a competition."

"Perhaps the glass was accidentally knocked over," suggested Jacques.

"Perhaps it was, but how do you explain the positioning of the bottles? That spacing is classic to lead your eye through from the foreground to the centre of the picture."

"Maybe the scene of crime officer was just lucky and got the right shot."

"No, Jacques, no. Look more carefully. The photo

encompasses the whole of the draining board which provides a natural boundary which actually creates a frame for everything else that is there so your gaze travels first to the objects and it remains there because of the boundary. It's very cleverly done!"

Jacques took the photo from her and studied it. "Yes, I see what you mean," he said, passing it across to Pelletier. "What else do you see?"

Beth, moved the pictures of the shared living and dining area into the centre of the magistrate's desk. The black brocade curtains in the room were firmly closed and a modern steel standard light in the corner was left on overlooking the circular glass-topped table.

"Was the light on, or did your people switch it on?"

"The light was on when we entered the property, Madame Samuels."

Beth frowned. "Where's her computer? If I owned the place, that is where I would work and why would the light be on if she hadn't been working before whatever it was that happened to her, happened?"

Jacques picked up the line of questioning as he scanned each of the photos in turn. "And what about her laptop and brief case? She had a dark blue briefcase which looked very smart and expensive?"

"They were not found at the apartment and are still missing. In fact, there was nothing of a personal nature in the apartment at all apart from the phone on the bedside table and a note on the floor in the bathroom," said Pelletier.

"That explains why her handbag is missing, then. That was going to be my next question," said Beth.

Jacques thought for a moment. "Not there... Because they were removed or because they were never there in the first place?" He looked at Pelletier.

"It's difficult to say at the moment, Jacques."

The magistrate smiled at Beth. "Thank you, Madame Samuels. You've raised some important questions and presented me with a very interesting point of view. I need to think all this through, but if she does have another address somewhere else, then we need to find it fast."

"And what about providing a positive identification of the body? Do you still need me to do that, Bruno?"

"Yes, if Madame Samuels has no objection, we'll go to the morgue now and then perhaps you could access the details of the victim's next of kin from your files at Vaux."

"I'll go to the apartment, Jacques, and start the measuring up for you. Come across when you can." Beth grabbed her camera bag and moved to the door.

Jacques picked up his phone and called Michelle from HR in the hope that she might be able to access the information they required using her remote system log-in.

monday, october 19th,
two weeks earlier

The operations area at Vaux Consulting was buzzing with noise and tension. Hélène's grating voice could be heard as she shouted at the admin team about missing a deadline and Madeleine was floating between the Director's office and her own. Jacques could not quite decide how productive she was being. He logged back in to his computer and moved straight to the new secret drive on the network. The surveillance camera was working. He exited and made a mental note to take his laptop home with him and view the footage that night.

His emails consisted mostly of documents copied to him for information only, so he focussed on the emails from the Finance area containing the phone records for all the company mobiles. These he printed out and started working through them. In his corner of the work area he could watch the others, make notes unobserved, work uninterruptedly, and seemingly be ignored by everyone else.

He noted that Aimée arrived later than usual that morning. Flicking back through his notebook he checked her previous arrival times, always around 8am or just after. He checked his watch and noted down 9.38am and the date.

As soon as Aimée got to her desk, Madeleine came out of her own office and stalked across the floor.

"About Friday, I don't want a repeat of your open defiance again."

The harshness in Madeleine's voice made Jacques look up, as had one or two other members of the team. Jacques watched as Aimée stopped undoing the buttons of her coat and looked at her boss, bewildered. "Excuse me?"

"On Friday when I phoned you and asked you for the team's latest costs analysis you were deliberately prevaricating. I had Édouard at one side of me, Roger Baudin, the Finance Director, at the other side of me and the key stakeholders from my client's company sat opposite me. When I ask you to do something, I expect you to do it."

"But you—"

"I've just given you an instruction, Aimée. Are you going to acknowledge it?"

The sharpness of Madeleine's tone brought a general hush to the whole of the work area and Aimée, eyes cast down, began to colour.

"Yes," she said in a whisper.

Jacques was about to step in and comment when Madeleine moved closer to Aimée.

"Don't make that mistake again." She swept around and marched back to her own desk.

Jacques recognised the venom in her voice. She'd once used the same tone on him when they had been together in Paris. He shook his head to rid himself of the memory and watched as Aimée took off her coat, threw it onto the unoccupied desk next to hers and slumped into her chair. To give her a few moments to compose herself, he went back to his work on the phone lists and noticed that a new envelope had been placed on the corner of his own desk. He opened it and laid out the single sheet of paper in front of him and studied the contents.

YOU'RE DABBLING IN THINGS THAT DON'T CONCERN YOU.

BACK OFF.

His immediate reaction was instinctive, he felt in his jacket pocket for an evidence bag but didn't find one. Picking it up using the very edge of the paper he replaced it in the envelope and slotted that into his bag as a wry smile crossed his face. *Someone is feeling pressured. I wonder who that can be?* He glanced around the room.

The pop-up from the diary on his computer reminded him that he had a meeting with Roger Baudin in 15 minutes. He logged out, collected his papers and ambled over to Aimée's desk.

"What was that all about?" Jacques pulled the chair from the empty desk closer to Aimée's and sat down.

"Nothing!" Aimée continued to stare at the list of emails in her in-box.

"I know Madeleine is your boss, but she should not be speaking to you in that tone of voice in front of the whole team."

Aimée shrugged. "It happens all the time, Jacques. And it's not just me, either."

He glanced at his watch. "I need to go, but can we talk about this later this afternoon?"

Aimée, a resigned smile on her face, nodded. "I'll see you in the small meeting room at three, then."

As Jacques replaced the chair he realised that Hélène had been watching him. Consciously keeping her in his peripheral vision as he moved through the desks he saw her get up and move across to Aimée's desk. He made a mental note to find out what that conversation was about when he met Aimée later.

Roger was alone in his office poring over some spreadsheets. His desk was immaculately tidy. Three perfectly sharpened coloured pencils sat side by side within easy reach and by his computer were two mobile phones.

"Come in, Jacques." He motioned him to the chair at the other side of his desk, folded the printouts over and placed them carefully in a black wire tray to one side. "So, how are you finding us here at Vaux?" The very briefest of smiles traversed his lean, tanned face.

"I'm very content here. However, this internal investigation means that I am probably making a lot of enemies very quickly."

"It has to be done. What can I help you with?"

Jacques opened his notebook. "You've been with the

company for fourteen years, I believe, and during that time you must have been involved in putting together plenty of bids."

Roger nodded. "I work on all the bids and it's myself, Alain and Édouard who make the final decisions about what a bid will look like immediately before it is submitted."

"So, if you wanted to leak important information to a competitor, you would be able to with surety about the data you provide and in the certain knowledge that you would be believed, probably without question."

Roger took a deep breath. "You could say that. But I wouldn't sabotage my own position in that way."

"You do know people at C and C Consulting, though?"

"Yes, my wife works for them. But we both make a point of leaving the work in our respective office space, Jacques."

"So, you never discuss the difficulties of the day with each other over dinner and perhaps and, without intending to, give away small pieces of important information?"

Roger smiled. "I see what you are getting at, but the answer is no."

"Do you spend time at events with people from C and C?"

"Naturally. I can't avoid my wife's colleagues in the same way that she can't avoid mine at such events. It's the way this business works, Jacques."

The silence between them tensed as Jacques scrutinised the face of the man opposite. His square jaw was set rigid, his blue eyes stared out steadily and unblinkingly. There was nothing to read.

You'd make a damn good professional poker player!

"And what about your briefcase and laptop? You do take them home with you?"

"Of course, but if you are going to accuse me of deliberately leaving my papers lying around or my laptop open with an important file on screen, then I can save you the time. My wife and I each have our own office space at home. She works in the smallest bedroom. We converted that space into an office for her six years ago, when she returned to work full-time. I have an office space in the attic. In summer, we occasionally can be found working in the summer house in the garden. Then she usually sits at the table inside and I work on the patio in front. We don't share our work. If we do work at home, we normally do so in separate rooms."

"And it's never occurred to you or your wife to search through each other's papers looking for useful information?"

Roger stared at him. "No," he said with finality. "We trust each other."

Jacques took a different tack. "The finances for both companies as a whole, Roger, are they healthy? I only ask because Alain has led me to believe that finding the source of the leaked information is critical to the continuance of this organisation."

Roger sat back and thought for a moment. "We're covering our costs but I can't see us making any large bonus payments this year. The cyber-attack last week will cost us a lot to clear as I am sure there will be a suit for reparations and, ultimately, I expect that we will lose that contract as soon as it is financially viable for our client to effect that. Internally, we need to make some efficiencies and we need to cut back on the excessive expenses bill. We've already tightened up on payment collection and we've reviewed and revised our payments structure. But I can't retro-fit these new policies to existing contracts, so the impact of that will only be felt in the coming months. But, if the speculation at the last Board meeting proves to be true...the costs arising from the cyber-attack can probably be met. That, of course, assumes that there are no other unforeseen events between now and the end of the current accounting year."

"These excessive expenses—"

The muffled sound of a phone ringing interrupted Jacques. He glanced at the phones on the desk, both of which were silent. Roger glanced at Jacques, a clear flicker of annoyance displayed on his face.

"I can leave if the call is important..."

Roger looked across to his jacket hanging from the stand in the corner by the door and shook his head. "It will be my wife. It will go to voicemail." He waited until the phone fell silent. "You were asking about the expense accounts," he prompted.

"Yes. Do you know what the exact problem is?" Jacques quickly jotted a note to remind himself to check all of Roger's phones on the printouts.

"The expenses are monitored and paid by our HR team. They manage the Vaux payroll for both companies and the expenses are paid into employees' bank accounts. It's company policy and has been for the last three years. However, I'm concerned that we are losing control and I've asked HR to look into the matter urgently. I suggest you talk to Michelle. She's the senior manager and is responsible for the internal payroll and her team administer the expenses system for all employees."

***

The hunting party from the previous week had left, and Beth was free to roam through the forest and capture shots of the bright autumnal display in the canopies of the deciduous trees. Early that morning there had been a hoar frost, giving the landscape and everything in it a glistening white sheen until the sun had become strong enough to melt it into a damp mist. Returning to the chalet later, she came across Gendarme Clergue as he walked up the D6 towards her.

"Some good shots, I hope," shouted Clergue as he reached her gate and waited for her to arrive.

"Yes. Would you like to come in for a coffee?"

He nodded his acceptance and followed her up the short path and into the house.

In the kitchen, she first put the coffee pot on the stove and then took off her coat, hung it over the back of a stool at the breakfast bar, and placed her camera bag on the seat.

Clergue remained standing and removed his cap. "I'm

afraid I have some news that you may find a little upsetting."

Beth took a breath and waited.

"It's about Fermier Delacroix. I'm very sorry to tell you that he died yesterday. He suffered a massive heart attack in hospital in Mende. Despite the doctor's best efforts, it proved impossible to revive him."

"I see." Beth sat down for a moment. "I had hoped I had been quick enough to ensure that he could be saved." She scraped her hand through her hair and sighed.

"There was nothing more that you could have done, Madame."

"But, there will be arrangements to make...and what about his family? Do they know?"

"He has a nephew in Canada, and we've contacted the Canadian police and asked them to ensure that he is informed. There's nothing for you to do."

The coffee signalled it was ready to be poured and Beth shook herself back to reality. "Sorry, umm... Whilst I didn't know Fermier Delacroix well, it's still a bit of a shock to hear that someone you know...knew, has died." To distract herself from the sad news she moved across to the cupboard for the cups and busied herself with the familiar and comforting but simple ritual of preparing and pouring the drinks for herself and her guest.

"So, that will mean a funeral here in the village, and please sit down, Gendarme Clergue."

"It's Thibault, Madame, now that my official business is concluded." A wide smile crossed his face as he added two heaped spoons of sugar to his cup.

"You'd better drop the Madame as well, then!" Beth cradled her cup in both hands to warm them. "It's a bit raw out there today, Thibault. Is it always like this at this time of year?"

"Often, yes. Nearer to Christmas we get the very fast winds of the Mistral blowing in from the north west and in January and February we often get snow." He gulped his coffee. "Are you planning to stay through the winter?"

"I hadn't given it that much thought, but I think I would like to be back in the UK for Christmas. To me there is only one place to be at Christmas and that's home." She sipped her drink and then placed her cup on the counter. "Delacroix's funeral? Will the whole village be there, do you think, or will it just be family?"

"It will be everyone. It would be considered an insult if you did not attend."

"I see. But what about Fermier Rouselle. He openly showed his dislike of Delacroix whilst he was alive. Will he be there too?"

"I would expect so. It will be his last opportunity to acknowledge that their feud over their shared boundary is at an end." The policeman smiled. "He might arrive late, but he will be there."

Beth grinned. "Village politics! I don't think I will ever understand them."

"Perhaps not, but, after the meeting with the *Maire* last week, I expect there will be lots of changes here in the next few years."

Beth smiled and nodded her agreement.

"What about you? Will you move here permanently?"

Beth studied his heavily jawed, but friendly face. "That's a very big question, Thibault, and it's something that I'm still giving a lot of serious thought to." She gazed out of the window for a few moments before replying. "Moving to another country on a permanent basis is a very daunting prospect."

He smiled at her. "If it helps you to make up your mind, I and most of the villagers here would welcome you as a resident."

"As would Jacques!"

***

The tension across the table at the *Drap d'Or* as Jacques and Philippe Chauvin, the IT Director at Vaux, decided on their choices from the lunch menu, made the waiter uneasy.

He stood, apprehensively looking from one to the other, his pen poised and order pad in hand.

Jacques rattled off his choices.

"I'll have the same," Philippe said, handing the waiter his menu.

"I thought I'd made myself very clear, Philippe. So why did you involve Alain?"

"I don't agree with what you are doing. I didn't agree when you first approached me about the extra surveillance camera being added into the network and I still don't agree." He toyed with the fork set out in front of him.

"So, rather than coming to me you went straight to Alain." He let the implied insult drift between them, but Philippe maintained his stony stare. "Who else knows?"

The waiter returned with a basket of bread and some wine which he was about to pour when he was waved away by Jacques. "Who else?"

"No-one."

"Are you certain of that?"

"I'm responsible for our IT system, Jacques, and all its surrounding security. I do know how to keep my mouth shut, and I'm very well aware of how to handle sensitive issues." His raised voice caused a look from the two businessmen at the next table. In the slight lull in the conversation Philippe smiled at the two men who returned their attention to their own meal.

Jacques nodded and filled their glasses with wine. In the awkward silence, they waited for their entrées and as soon as the waiter had left, Jacques began working through his, now well-rehearsed, questions. By the time the coffee was served, Jacques had yet another member of the Vaux organisation who had the means and the opportunity to effect the transfer of information to a rival company, but who lacked the motive and who consistently maintained his innocence.

Deciding to trust Chauvin, Jacques changed the subject. "Philippe, I know we didn't begin on the best of terms today, but I need your help."

Chauvin dropped a cube of sugar into his cup. "Go on."

"This investigation is turning out to be very complex. But try as I might, I can't find any clear leads to follow. But what I do know is that all the documentation that has apparently been leaked has been stored on the office network. I don't understand exactly how the network is constituted nor how it really works. But my instinct is suggesting to me that I might be missing something…"

"You want my help to understand what we do?"

"Yes. I'm not sure what questions I need you to answer at the moment."

Philippe grinned, drained his coffee cup and put it back in the saucer.

"Only too pleased to help you with that. I've got a meeting this afternoon until three, so we can talk after that in my office if that's convenient."

Jacques shook his head. "I'd rather we talked out of the office in this instance. There are too many eyes watching what I'm doing in the Vaux buildings."

"I'll meet you at Bar de la Paix in Badaroux at seven," he said as he glanced at his watch. "I'll get the bill, Jacques, and I have to be back for my meeting."

Jacques nodded and took his first sip of coffee. The table next to his was now empty and when he looked around the dining room, Philippe was making his way to the bar to pay.

His coat collar pulled up against the cold drizzle, Jacques returned to his own desk. Admitting to himself that he was no further forward was especially disappointing. Conjuring up what he might say to Alain and Édouard at his meeting with them the next day made him feel ill at case. There were too many suspects who could have breached security, but as yet, he could not identify a single reason for any one of them to do so.

Someone knows. Someone's guilty.

He let himself into the building and nodded to Luc, the security guard who was on duty at the desk in the lobby. There were other lines of enquiry to follow up and further background checks to be made, and the overheard conversation to check into. Wearily his feet took the stairs one by one and the only glimmer of satisfaction came from the fact that, by the end of their meal he had at least managed to make his peace with Philippe.

As soon as Aimée had closed the door on the small meeting room, the tears pricked the back of her eyes.

"I have had it," she said as she slumped down in the chair opposite Jacques. "I've had enough!" A tear trickled down her cheek.

"Let's start with that conversation between you and Madeleine this morning. What was that all about?" Jacques pushed his notebook aside deciding to just listen.

"That? That wasn't about work; that was all about Madeleine! On Friday, I was very busy drafting the strategy and plan detailing how the internal announcement required for our client would be made. Then Madeleine rang and asked for the updated team cost analysis. It's something that I do every Friday. The revised costs are filed on the network and are always there by 4pm at the latest. That's the agreed deadline and she knows that."

"And did you remind her of that?"

"I tried to tell her that it was on my list of things to do that day. But she wouldn't listen. She just interrupted me with another demand. I started to tell her that I would be picking up that task next. I only had about another hour's work to complete on the strategy, so the revised costings would have been online before lunch and therefore well before the deadline. But she just would not let me speak. She cut me off and demanded that I do the costings that morning." Aimée frowned. "It was such a stupid thing to say because those costings are always done on a Friday."

Jacques reached for his notebook and pen. "Can you remember exactly what she said?"

Aimée thought for a moment. "I think she said, 'I want it done now' and then she asked me, 'Is that clear?' in that really harsh demanding tone of hers."

Jacques nodded. "Madeleine demanded a piece of work that she already knew you would complete on Friday by an already agreed deadline and this work was something that was always done on a weekly basis. Have you ever missed that deadline before?"

"Hmm...only once and that was way back in May."

"Was there anything in that conversation on Friday that might have led you to believe that Madeleine wanted you to email the data to her straight away?"

"No, she never actually asked for that, and when I tried to offer to do that for her she interrupted me again and then the phone went dead. I assumed that she had cut me off."

"Did she have her laptop with her?"

"I think so. She copied me into some emails later that evening, so she must have taken it home. Also, I found about half a dozen emails from her in my in-box the next morning. The Friday morning when she called me. Last Friday."

"And the conversation with Hélène just after I left?"

"That! That was a demonstration of the simpering, trying-to-be-your-friend-but-oh-so-poisonous, Hélène! You don't have to worry about that, Jacques. I know what she's doing."

"But I don't, and I would like to know."

Aimée sighed. "She offered to take over the work on the costings as I *needed help*, apparently. I'm looking *very tired*, it seems."

"Did you give her the work to do?"

"No! Nor would I! The updated costings will be there on Friday, as usual, and I will do them. Had I agreed to let Hélène do it she would have gone running to Madeleine and told her I can't cope with my workload."

"You don't know that for certain."

"Yes, I do! Because that's what she did last time. It may have taken me a few months to work out exactly what game she was playing, but I'm not completely stupid, Jacques. I'm not about to let her humiliate and manipulate me like that again."

"Last time?" He dumped his pen on top of his notebook and waited.

Aimée shook her head. "You don't really want to hear about that, do you?"

"Aimée, this investigation is about security leaks and so far, all I have are plenty of people with means and opportunity but no apparent reason to want to sabotage their employer's business. I'm now looking into everyone's background to see if there is something there that might help me. But I'm also taking a very close look at the personal dynamics between the team members. And…I'm not liking what I'm finding."

Jacques watched as her expression moved from irritation to a concerned frown.

"I see." She checked her watch and, face a composed blank, looked him in the eye and said, "Last May, the costings were not updated on time because Hélène was sick for the first three days of that week. I picked up a critical piece of work that had been assigned to her but had not yet been started. It was a strategy document that was supposed to have been at the first draft stage by the end of the week. I determined that the strategy document took precedence. That meant the update of the costings would be left until the last minute and done on Friday and, if necessary, estimates would be used if I could not get the precise data. On the Thursday morning of that week, Hélène came in late;, it was about eleven, I think. Anyway, she came in claiming that she still wasn't well but knew that she had a key piece of work to complete. Despite the urgency of her work, she spent her time in Madeleine's office and then they both went out to lunch. That afternoon she came to me and told me that the work on the strategy had been re-assigned to her by Madeleine. I'd almost—"

"And how did you feel about that?" Jacques interrupted her flow and she fell into, what appeared to him, a confused and momentary silence.

"Ummm… Annoyed, I think. Inwardly, I was very annoyed, as I'd almost completed the work. Instead, I suggested that we swop tasks and that she take on the costings update and analysis in place of the work on the strategy. I made the suggestion in good faith, and I certainly had no intention of letting her waltz in and take full credit for all the work I'd already done. The following Monday, Madeleine came to my desk and, in front of the rest of the team, told me I needed help with my workload. That I should assign various items of work to Hélène and that I should consider attending a time-management course." Aimée stood and moved to the door. "I know what she's doing, Jacques, and I'm not playing her game, but that doesn't stop me getting fed up or pissed off with the constant shifts in her moods and attitude." Wrenching the door open, she swept out of the room and slammed it behind her.

Jacques stared out of the window as he assimilated what he'd just heard. *Someone else who uses lies and deception to achieve their own ends.* He frowned as he wondered exactly what it was that Hélène was seeking to achieve other than to undermine a colleague. *I wonder how long this has been going on.*

Snapping out of his thoughts, he collected his notebook and the few papers he had with him and returned to his desk. Digging out Hélène's personal file, he leafed through the documents until he found her application for employment with Vaux. He copied the details of her last three previous employers into his notebook.

***

A tall thin man in a dark green hoodie loped along the path by the river. It was a favourite haunt in July and August when he could watch the women playing tennis in their short dresses.

He pulled the sleeve of his jacket across his face and sniffed. Squatting down behind a tree and, facing the river, he pulled out his phone and checked the time. He wouldn't have to wait long. But he didn't like waiting when there was nothing or no-one to watch. He looked around and then sent a text.

Where R U
Luciole

A few moments later his phone buzzed as a response arrived.

B there soon. Have got the money. Have got a job for you.

The man let out a loud hollow laugh and turned his phone off. He'd be patient, he decided. But only for the next couple of minutes.

***

Unable to sleep, Jacques quietly got out of bed and slipped out of the room and down the spiral staircase. In the kitchen, he poured himself a glass of water and sauntered through to the dining area to watch the dawn break over the valley and the mountains beyond. The sky was mostly grey and covered by blanket clouds, so he moved into the central space in the chalet and stood and looked at it in detail.

Never noticed that before!

He continued to survey the beams across the high ceiling and up in the roof space. The door to the master bedroom was closed as usual and he fleetingly wondered why Beth would not use the room. It was much larger than the one upstairs and more comfortable, with access to the covered patio at the back of the chalet. *Maybe she'll change her mind when she decides to move here permanently.* He frowned. *If she moves here…*

He went back to the dining room and, seeing his bag propped against the leg of the table, he realised that he had not looked at the footage from the new camera covering the smoking area. He quickly unpacked his laptop from his bag

84

and logged in to the Vaux network.

Most of the footage was of a blank screen with the odd car or person moving in and out of the underground car park. At one point, a lean man in a dark coloured hoodie loped just within view of the camera, looked towards the roller door on the entrance to the car park and then moved out of sight. *An opportunist probably.* There were a few short conversations of no particular note and then, after most of the staff had gone home, he found himself watching the screen with great interest. He stopped, rewound, got out his notebook and pressed play so that he could go through the whole scene in detail.

surveillance camera footage

Hélène lights her cigarette, pulls her coat around her, steps back and huddles into the concrete pillar that supports the metal grill above the entrance to the underground car park at the back of the building.

19/10/2009 18.36.16

The grey screen remains still with only the white of the time and date field in the bottom right corner ticking the seconds away.

19/10/2009 18.37.15

The roller door begins to rise on cue as the sensor inside picks up an entity. Bending low under the still rising door, Aimée steps out and comes into view.

19/10/2009 18.38.01

"Aimée! Sneaking out for a quick fag! I didn't know you smoked."

Aimée turns, a startled look on her face, full on to camera. "I don't."

19/10/2009 18.38.15

"We've not had much of a chance to talk recently. Let's catch up and chat. Yes?"

"I'm meeting someone." Aimée turns to leave.

19/10/2009 18.38.28

"Anyone I know?"

Aimée steps back and gives Hélène a disdainful look.

19/10/2009 18.38.35

"Boyfriend? Is it Nicolas? I did know you were seeing each, you know. Not Nicolas? Shame."

Aimée stands her ground and folds her arms, her face impassive.

19/10/2009 18.38.54

"Dumped you, has he, Aimée? So sad, you deserve to be —"

"It's 18.38, Hélène." Aimée shows her watch to Hélène after glancing at it herself.

19/10/2009 18.39.13

"This is not the office. This is my time. And you know what, Hélène, as Madeleine said to me all those months ago, when I first got here, I don't have to put up with all the shit that you dish out. And I'm not going to. Alright?"

19/10/2009 18.39.25

Aimée turns to go but Hélène moves into view and grabs her by the arm.

"What does that mean?"

19/10/2009 18.39.37

"Exactly what it says." Aimée's face is angry.

"You're lying! Madeleine would never have said that about me."

19/10/2009 18.39.51

Aimée looks at her colleague. "You really do believe that, don't you?" Looking at her arm. "Take your filthy paw off my sleeve." Aimée glowers.

19/10/2009 18.40.03

Hélène releases her grip.
"I know you're lying."

19/10/2009 18.40.12

87

"Then you're a complete fool, because I can quote the exact time and day when that was said to me."

19/10/2009 18.40.26

"I can be so precise because it was the moment that I lost all respect for Madeleine as a person and a manager. I was so appalled at her 'advice' as she called it, that I noted down her words in my diary immediately after that meeting.

19/10/2009 18.40.44

"And everything I've seen and been subjected to since then has not made me change my opinion of either of you one jot. I know what you are doing."

19/10/2009 18.41.00

Hélène stubs out her cigarette.
"I don't know what you're talking about, Aimée. I know you're having problems keeping up with the work and I'm just offering to give you a chance—"

19/10/2009 18.41.16

"Hah! You! Offering me a chance? To what, Hélène? To fall into yet another one of your little traps? You're even more delusional than I gave you credit for."

19/10/2009 18.41.28

Aimée makes to leave.
"Wait."

19/10/2009 18.41.34

"Now what?"
Hélène moves further into view and lights another cigarette. She tosses the spent match into the sand in the circular ash-can.

19/10/2009 18.41.52

"I'm trying to help you, Aimée." She moves forward and further into view, puts her arm across her colleague's shoulder and smiles.

19/10/2009 18.42.08

"I know you've missed your milestone on the plan for completion of the Communications Strategy and that this will come out at the board meeting on Tuesday."

19/10/2009 18.42.29

Aimée shrugs the arm away. "Do you, now?" Aimée crosses her arms and nods. "And how did you reach that conclusion?"

19/10/2009 18.42.43

Hélène puts her head on one side, a wide smile crosses her face. "It's not difficult, Aimée. All the files are on the F drive in the relevant folders. You don't have exclusive access, you know."

19/10/2009 18.42.59

Aimée, face impassive, stares at her colleague and remains silent.

"Of course, I had to let Madeleine know that you were about to let the whole team down. She has our reputation as top notch managers who always deliver on time and on budget to consider."

19/10/2009 18.43.36

"Yes, of course you did! Like I said, I don't have to put up with the shit that you dish out. I know it was you who changed the letter to Nicolas Durand and then tried to pin it on me. Aimée pauses.

19/10/2009 18.43.51

"I know it was you who deliberately steered the client's staff I'm working with in the wrong direction." Aimée moves closer to Hélène.

19/10/2009 18.44.03

"I know it was you who consciously engineered the conversation that Édouard overheard."

19/10/2009 18.44.16

"And way back in May, I know it was you who gave the costing analysis to someone that you knew did not have the expertise to complete the task."

19/10/2009 18.44.31

"I know what you are doing, Hélène. I know." Aimée face in full view smiles. "Just watch what happens next." She turns and moves out of camera.

19/10/2009 18.44.46

Hélène comes into full view and shouts after Aimée. "Don't walk away from me. Don't you dare walk away from me. Aimée…" Breathing heavily, she looks out of view.

19/10/2009 18.45.01

Turning full face to the camera, she stabs her half-smoked cigarette into the sand. "Bitch!" She keys in the entrance code to activate the mechanism for the roller door.

19/10/2009 18.45.14

tuesday, october 20th

"You're up early today." Beth, in her dressing gown, fresh from her morning shower, wrapped her arms around Jacques' neck as she looked over his shoulder at the screen on his laptop.

"You smell nice," he said as he gently caressed her face with his left hand.

"Some new conditioner I thought I'd try." She planted a light kiss on his cheek.

"Oh no, you don't! I'm not finished with you yet." He caught her wrist as she began to move away, pulled her round to face him and held her there. "There's some coffee left in the pot if you want it or I can make you some fresh or…"

"Nice idea." She grinned and then glanced at the laptop. "Haven't you got an important meeting today? And it doesn't matter about the coffee."

"You're right, and I do need to be fully prepared for the presentation to Alain and Édouard. What's wrong with a whiteboard and a detailed discussion? My previous investigations never needed computer presentations."

Beth winked at him. "That's a great set of slides you've got there!" She moved to the fridge to get some juice.

"You should know; you put them together for me! What are you doing today?" His attention back on the screen he scrolled through the slides one last time.

"This morning, I'm meeting with the couple who are getting married next month, so I can drop you off at Vaux if you want. Then I'm having lunch with Old Thierry and then —"

"You've decided what you want to do about his offer?"

The final slide checked, he closed down the programme and the laptop.

Her mouth full of croissant, Beth nodded. Jacques waited for her to respond, but she just picked up her glass of juice, the remainder of her pastry, took another bite and went up to the bedroom to get dressed.

He grinned as she gestured that she was eating. "Alright, keep eating and ignore me! I hope it goes well with Thierry," he shouted after her. "And don't bother about the lift, I'll take the bike." He disconnected the laptop from the mains and began to pack it into his bag.

Édouard Vaux was a heavily-built man in comparison with his younger brother. Jacques guessed that these differences in colouring and build meant that each brother strongly favoured only one of their respective parents.

"Are you saying that you have no leads at all?" Édouard pulled at the stiff cuffs of his pristine white shirt.

"No, I'm saying that I have a number of suspects that I need to narrow down further."

"Either you have leads, suspects or not. Which is it?" His tone hardened.

Jacques shifted in his chair. "I have suspects who have the means and the opportunity but as yet I can find no motive."

"No. The answer is no, then."

Jacques looked from Édouard to Alain but received no encouragement or support. He cleared his throat and acquiesced. "If that is your definition, then, no."

"You came highly recommended, Jacques. I expected far greater progress than this." He sifted through the presentation notes he had in front of him and pushed them to one side. "Alain and I need to talk. Please leave us."

Jacques hesitated. Alain gave him the slightest of nods, and Jacques collected his notes and laptop and moved towards the door. As he left the room, Mademoiselle Lapointe took a split second to lift her head and smile and then continued with her note-taking.

As Jacques made his way back to his desk, he mentally kicked himself for not taking a stronger line with the older brother. Slumping down in his chair, he wondered why Alain hadn't given him the support he had expected whenever Édouard questioned or demeaned his contentions and current suppositions. But then it was Édouard, through his assistant, that had proved particularly illusive and difficult in agreeing to a time to be interviewed. They both have means and opportunity, he reminded himself. Running his hands through his hair, he resolved to move them both to the top of his list of possible suspects.

But why? Why would one or both of them seek to destroy their own company? What do they gain by doing that?

As he took his place at his desk in the almost empty operations area he noticed a pile of post and began to sift through it. The last envelope had a typed label on it and his instinct told him that this was the only piece of post that he really needed to open.

Inside was a single sheet of paper with a very clear message.

YOU JUST DON'T LISTEN, DO YOU?
NEXT TIME IT WON'T BE A WARNING.

Jacques looked around but, of the few people in the room, all were working. Staring at computer screens, on the telephone or engrossed in clerical work of some sort. He carefully replaced the sheet of paper in the envelope and put it into the same pocket in his bag as the first one. On hearing Alain's voice as he left the board room, Jacques made his decision. Collecting his coat and bag, he cleared his desk and followed the others out on to the landing and down the stairs. Jacques finally caught up with his boss on the street outside.

Twenty minutes later, in the quiet confines of Alain's office, Jacques waited whilst Alain stared at the two threatening letters on his desk. "Can you check for finger prints?"

"No. I'm no longer on the force. If you want to pay a small fortune to the appropriate laboratory, then yes, we can get these letters checked. But I would guess that whoever has done this has been careful and will probably have left no trace or at least not enough for us to narrow down the list of suspects. Even if we can get any trace of fingerprints from them, because this is an internal matter, there's no guarantee that we can match them with anyone on the police database. Something else to which I no longer have access. We would also have to finger print everyone in both companies to see who matches any traces on those notes. Are you sure you want to waste resources on doing that?"

Alain shook his head and slumped down in his chair. "Tell me what you think this means?"

"That someone is feeling uncomfortable by my constantly asking questions. I need to keep up the pressure and to do that I need you to convince your brother that my approach is the right one." Jacques sat back in his chair and watched his boss. Alain stared at his desk and said nothing.

"I also need you to convince your brother that, both he and Mademoiselle Lapointe are also under consideration and that, like you, they cannot be excluded from my investigation. You need to impress upon him that I must question him. You might want to tell him that I won't be restricting my questions to the current investigation. I will be asking him about the difficulties between the personnel in his team and the open intimidation that exists between them."

Alain did not respond immediately and his face showed no indication of his reaction or what it might be. He passed the letters across to Jacques and picked up his phone.

"I'll talk to Mademoiselle Lapointe. If anyone can persuade him, it will be her."

The late afternoon sun provided the final remnants of warmth as it descended behind the high peaks to the far west of the village. Along with the deepening chill and growing dusk came the delighted squeals of Pierre Mancelle as he let his red bicycle freewheel down the slope past Beth's chalet, arms and legs out-stretched. As he reached the point where Delacroix's vehicle had crashed he grabbed his handle bars, braked hard and let out a loud scrunching noise as he then faked his own accident. Spread-eagled on the damp grass, he breathed his imaginary last breath and then immediately jumped up and transmogrified into Gendarme Clergue. Right hand outstretched in the shape of a gun and supported at the wrist by his left hand he put his pretend cattle out their distress. The recoil on the police pistol he believed he was holding was accompanied by the appropriate vocal sound effect. Satisfied he'd done a good job he replaced his trusty weapon in its holster. On his bike once more, the whole mini drama began again as he set off along the bottom road into the village, up the steep track to the top road and left towards the fork with the road that crossed the col to Rieutort.

The third replay of the scenario took a different turn. He joined the road where the accident had occurred a few moments after Beth had sped past in her car. As he came level with her chalet, he saw her outside taking a large box out of the boot. He turned into her drive and cycled the few metres to her front door.

"Junior Gendarme Mancelle on patrol, Madame Samuels." A wide smile on his face, he saluted smartly.

"Pierre…sorry, Gendarme Mancelle, how are you?" Beth moved another box onto the front porch.

"I'm going back to school tomorrow. My medicine is finished today so Maman and the doctor said I'm better now."

Beth smiled at the simplicity of his view of life. "That's very good news. And does Maman know where you are?"

"Oh yes. I told her I was going on patrol and she said that I've got to be back home by four."

She glanced at her watch, there was another half hour of freedom for him yet. "Oh, well, if I phone her and let her know you're here do you think she will let you give me a helping hand with all these boxes?"

He nodded as Beth took out her phone and dialled. A few moments later, assent given, Beth opened the door of the car to reveal a pile of box files laid out across the rear seats.

"Do you think you could take those files into the snug for me and put them on the floor in front of the book cases?"

Another smart salute. "Happy to help Madame Samuels."

Beth placed two box files, one on top of the other and gently rested them on his proffered forearms. Then she picked up the first box. "Follow me, and as we're working together, now Pierre, I think you'd better call me Beth."

The boy stopped dead in his tracks on the top step of the porch. "Maman says I'm not allowed to do that. She say's I can only call grown-ups Monsieur or Madame."

"OK." Beth balanced the box unsteadily on one arm as she used her spare hand to unlock the door and push it open. "Well, we can't go against what Maman says, can we?" She stood with her foot holding the door back to let the youngster through. "How about you call me Madame…?" She was about to suggest her own shortened name and then realised that, whilst an adult used to speaking English could cope with the final digraph, a boy of six may not be so capable. As she placed the heavy box on the floor in the corner at the far side of the hearth, she heard in her mind his young voice pronounce her name in the standard French manner. A smirk spread across her face as the mental picture of the bordello keeper in a Victorian gothic novel that she had read recently came into her mind. *Hmm, Madame Bette is perhaps not a good choice!*

"I think it might be better to call me Madame Elizabeth," she suggested, pronouncing her full name as a French person would.

"Like the Queen in England?" He offered her the box files, his eyes wide in wonderment. "Do you really have the same name as the Queen?"

To hide her amusement, she took the files and spent a few moments arranging them one on top of the other.

"Yes, and there the similarity ends," she said as she

shepherded the boy back out to the car.

Another half-dozen trips and all of Old Thierry's photos, negatives, boxes of equipment, cameras and lenses were safely stored on the floor in the snug and Pierre's curiosity finally got the better of him as he lifted the flap on the nearest box.

"Are you going to the be like Old Thierry now?"

Beth let out a light chuckle and joined him, crossed legged, on the floor. "Yes," she said as she opened another box, "I suppose you could say that."

"Wow!" Uninvited, Pierre began delving into the box and lifted out a lens with one hand and a small camera with the other and held them up for his detailed examination.

"Careful!" Beth retrieved the lens and placed it behind her on the sofa. "Some of this equipment is very delicate and expensive, Pierre, so we need to treat it with great respect. And that camera you're holding, is from the 1960s and, to a collector, it could be worth quite a few Euros."

Cradling the object in both hands, he gave it to her. "You mean a lot of money, like hundreds and hundreds of Euros?"

"Perhaps not that many…but I really don't know, Pierre. There's an auction site on the internet that I use and I've agreed with Old Thierry that everything in this box will be sold." Beth opened the back of the camera and checked the film advance lever and the shutter. "This is where the 35mm film would go," she said, showing the empty inside to Pierre. Then she snapped the back shut, focussed the lens and peered through the view finder, lined up a shot of the boy and clicked.

"Does it still work?"

"I'd say so but there's no film inside so I can't be sure." She shrugged. "Do you want to know how to use it?"

Pierre nodded and within moments both of them were lost in the detail of lining up shots, focussing on the subject and how the development process worked. Beth had a willing pupil and, unexpectedly, she found herself to be a capable teacher until a gentle knock on the front door brought both of them back to reality.

Marie, arriving much later than intended, claimed her child and returned home.

***

In the shadows created by the trees, a tall, thin man in a dark green hoodie squatted and watched and waited. Seeing the woman and the boy leave, he knew that the only other person in the chalet was alone. He flicked yet another cigarette butt onto the damp ground behind him and thought about giving up and heading back to Mende, but he had to know if this was the right place. No-one had told him anything about any other occupants of the house. But it was a wooden building. An old hunting lodge. He liked that. He was looking forward to doing this job.

An hour or so later, a motorbike pulled off the road and up the driveway. The man noted down the registration plate on the back of the scrap of paper on which the name and address of the chalet had been written. As he watched, Jacques Forêt parked the BSA, removed his helmet and went inside. The man leered as he recognised his true target.

wednesday, october, 21st

"Thanks for agreeing to see me," said Jacques as he walked into Édouard's office and sat opposite his interviewee. His eyes automatically swept across the desk in front of him which was covered in papers. At one corner were a set of three photo frames and Jacques assumed they would be of family but made a mental note to check if he got the chance.

"I'm a suspect, I believe," Édouard said, lips pursed and his expression and tone conveying his extreme displeasure.

"Everyone is until they are eliminated. That's how I work. Your brother employed me because of the way I work and because of my record of successes."

Édouard bristled but said nothing.

"I'd like to begin with something from your past." Jacques produced the copy of the torn portion of the letter that he had found in Alain's personnel file and placed it on top of the papers on the desk directly in Édouard's sightline. "According to Alain, you can explain what this means."

"You have no right!" Édouard blustered. "You have no right to question me about this!" Slamming his chair against the wall, he got up and marched to the window and remained there for a few moments.

Jacques was surprised that a man of his heavy build could move with such speed and agility. With Édouard's back towards him, Jacques took the opportunity to quietly move the angle of the photo frames and check their contents. Each one was of Édouard with some other business colleagues, all smiling and shaking hands. Seconds passed as Jacques waited patiently.

Édouard turned, hands in his trouser pockets and a broad smile on his face. "I can't see what a fantasy from the past

99

can have to do with your current investigation. Shall we move on?" He resumed his position at his desk and looked Jacques in the eye.

"Luckily, I'm the ex-policeman here and I can see that this…fantasy, as you call it, may have a bearing on this investigation. If this isn't a fantasy and if there was a child, that child would now be in his or her late thirties. That child might be in this organisation working for you or possibly against you. That child might be the person I need to find."

"It was a long time ago." Édouard placed his elbows on the desk and steepled his chubby hands as he let out a deep sigh. "But I see that you do have a point." After a moment, he continued. "There were about a dozen letters, I think. The first one arrived late in 1971."

"Can you remember the exact date or the month?"

"It's almost forty years ago, perhaps October or November, I can't be sure."

Jacques made a note. "And do you still have it?"

"No. I read it and then threw it in the bin. I didn't know the woman. As far as I can remember, I had never met her and I just assumed she had wrongly addressed the envelope."

"Can you remember anything of the content?"

Édouard smiled. "It was the sort of thing a teenager might write to a boy she had just met, that's all I remember."

"If it was a genuine mistake that the letter was sent to you, why did you not return it?"

Édouard shrugged. "That didn't occur to me. Maybe I wanted to save her the embarrassment. I don't know what was in my mind then, and now I'm not absolutely sure that there was a return address on the envelope. But I do know that I threw it away."

"And the other letters?"

"There were a couple more in the same vein, maybe three. All of which I ripped up and threw in the bin. And, no, I can't remember the detail of the content nor the precise dates when each one arrived."

Jacques nodded. "OK. You said there were about twelve letters, the first three or four you destroyed. That still leaves up to six or seven more and the fragment of the one that was kept. What can you tell me about those?"

"It was in January or February of the following year when the next one arrived, and I think that was the first one that definitely had a return address on the envelope. I didn't bother to open it. I just sent it back. It was the same with the ones that followed after that."

Jacques stared at the wall behind Édouard and thought for a moment. "Why keep this one letter? If the others had either been destroyed or returned, why keep this one? And where is the rest of the letter?"

Édouard picked up the photocopy of the fragment and read it. He handed the page to Jacques. "I don't know."

"What don't you know? Why it was kept or where the rest of the letter is? What?"

Jacques detected Édouard's slight recoil in response to his more forceful tone. A tone that he had deliberately employed. When there was no answer, he continued more quietly. "I have another question for you, Édouard. If you weren't reading the letters at this point, who was?" He paused again. "Who read this one and decided it should be kept?"

"Damn it, man! I don't know." He thumped his hand on his desk. "But what I do know, and I am absolutely certain of this, is that there was no child. There was no child because I have never been to Ireland and the return address was in Ireland."

Yet another new dimension to this case! Jacques narrowed his eyes and searched his interviewee's face for the faintest indication of a lie. But there was nothing. Édouard's colour had paled and his dark eyes held a cold and determined stare.

It was Jacques who broke the heavy silence. "And that's why you maintain it is a fantasy, is that right?"

"*I know* it is a fantasy," he said, underlining the first two words with a raised and strident voice.

Jacques decided to move on.

"Your connections with C and C Consulting, what are they?" He relaxed back in his chair and rested his left ankle on his right knee.

"I know all of the senior team there, have done for quite a while. It's how things work in my business, Jacques." There was a cold snide smile to accompany his retort.

Jacques, taking his time, consulted the notes he'd made the previous week. "And by that I presume you mean the company directors? The senior project managers?"

"Of course, their internal organisation is very similar to mine and we have worked jointly on projects in the past."

"So…it is possible that any one of your people could be passing information to C and C?"

"Yes, it's possible, but I don't accept that that is the case here. My people are loyal to this company, as am I." He glanced at his watch. "I have another appointment. Are there any final questions?"

"Your project team, would you say they were a happy team?"

"I would say they work very hard for the excellent rewards they get in terms of salary, expenses and bonuses."

"You haven't noticed any animosity within the team?"

Édouard frowned. "Why? Should I? Are you telling me how to manage my team now?"

Jacques had further questions, but instead he flipped his notebook shut and put it in his jacket pocket and stood. "1971, you'd be, how old?"

"I was 21."

Jacques retrieved his copy of the letter fragment from the desk and moved to the door. "Old enough, then. Even if you hadn't visited Ireland, you would still have been old enough to have fathered a child born the following year." He grinned and closed the door behind him.

Back at his desk in the operations area, Jacques picked up a call from a company in Rouen. He listened attentively. After a moment, he put the phone on the desk and went through a pile of post until he found a large envelope addressed to him, marked *private and confidential*. Picking up the phone, he confirmed that the package had been received.

Opening the envelope, he pulled out the documents sufficiently to assure himself they were what he had asked for and then replaced them and put the package in the top of drawer of his desk which he locked. He would examine those papers when in his own building across the road, and when no-one else was around.

His next meeting was with Michelle in HR as had been suggested by Roger Baudin. He made his way to the small meeting room on the third floor to find her waiting for him with various sets of papers and printouts spread across the table.

"Sorry to keep you waiting, Michelle, and I'll try not to take up too much of your time."

Michelle nodded and smiled.

"Roger Baudin made some remarks the other day that have prompted my enquiry, and clearly a good deal of work for you," he said, scanning all the documents on the table. "I understand there is some sort of credit card system in place for expenses, and if you can explain it to me, then I can decide whether it has any bearing on my current investigation."

"It's fairly straightforward. We have individual internal credit cards for the senior staff to use. Our managers use their cards when they need to set up lunch meetings at company expense with either existing clients or potential new ones. But those costs are only covered up to a fixed limit and for some items, such as wine, we only pay for a fixed quantity. Anything over that limit has to be paid for by the individual concerned."

Jacques frowned. "How do you keep a track of that?"

"It's not as difficult as it sounds. A lot of the managers pay the whole bill with the company credit card on the day, then list the actual costs to be reimbursed on the expenses claim for that week or month. So, where a second bottle of wine, which is not covered, for example, has been ordered and already paid for on the card, it is itemised on the expenses claim as a refund due to Vaux. These managers will also be claiming mileage as well as other expenses for visits out of town and that refund due to us would be recovered by being off-set against the other outstanding expenses due and any balance remaining is paid direct to their bank account a few days later."

"That seems straight forward enough." Jacques frowned. "Forgive my policeman's instincts, but how do you know everyone is being as honest as the system requires them to be?"

Michelle grimaced. "Your instincts are right, I'm afraid. The reality is that we don't know if everyone is being scrupulously honest or not. The costs across all of the expense budget heads have been steadily rising over the last three years. It's something that Roger is concerned about and that's why he asked me to have a look and see if I could identify what was happening..."

Jacques waited as she paused in thought. "And?" he prompted eventually.

"I really don't know if I should tell you this yet, but I'm thinking that some of the managers are using the credit card to fund their anticipated monthly expenses in advance."

"Do you have any examples?" Jacques' mind was working fast and shooting off in a cascade of different directions all at once.

"From the few examples I've looked at so far, I think there are some mismatches between what should be claimed and what has actually been paid on the card—"

"Misappropriation? How widespread?"

Michelle hesitated. "Umm... I want to give my colleagues the benefit of the doubt, so, no, I won't call it misappropriation. I'm sure it is by genuine error rather than by deliberate calculation. But I can see that the temptation is there."

Jacques nodded. "Error means it will happen once or twice in a year. Misappropriation means that it happens on a regular basis. So, which is it, and how much are we talking about?"

Michelle pushed the sleeves of her dark green dress part way up her forearms and began to delve into one of the piles of paper she had brought. "I don't know how much, Jacques, but I can show you one account that seems to be a particular problem." Having located the documents she wanted, she spread them out in front of Jacques, and then came round to his side of the table.

"I've highlighted the entries that are of concern. This is the credit card payment for a lunch for four," she pointed to a line on the first computer printout, "and here is the actual expenses claim. The lunch is simply itemised as a single entry for the amount claimed, and this is the actual expenses total paid. If you look through these sheets, you'll see that there is a regular item for lunch for a similar amount. This means that there is a regular payment of around €250 per month, and if you look at this sheet," she took another document, "you'll see this has been the case for every month since April this year."

Jacques glanced from one sheet to another and mentally totalled up the possible overpayment to date and across a whole year. He wondered how wide the practise was.

"But why are you so sure that this is not a genuine claim?"

Michelle presented the final piece of documentation. "If you look at the actual claims you'll see that there are no receipts for the items I've highlighted. For the similar amounts that are not highlighted there is a receipt – a very genuine receipt – and, in each instance, we have recovered the cost of extra wine from expenses due in those weeks. And there's something else, Jacques. The managers can use their credit cards to obtain cash from cash machines." She drew his attention to an entry on one of the printouts. "That's what has happened here," she said.

Jacques got up and moved to the window as he considered why someone would use such a method to unlawfully gain income, knowing full well that it was only a matter of time before they were found out.

He turned to Michelle. "This strategy to supplement a salary is either reckless or driven by desperation," he said. "Surely everyone in the whole group knows that you check expenses claims."

Michelle grimaced and glanced down at the floor. "You're right; everyone does know that expenses claims are checked. But everyone also knows that in the last two weeks of every month when we are running payrolls, our priority is to ensure that those payments to our clients are absolutely correct. Then our priority for system checks is on the payroll, not the expenses claims. And if we look at the example I've highlighted for you and check the dates of the submitted expenses claims, you will see that, all apart from two, were submitted in the last two weeks of each month."

Jacques checked the claims forms for himself. "That means it is a deliberate and calculated strategy, Michelle. In my book that's misappropriation at the very least."

Michelle frowned and nodded. "I knew that's what you'd say, Jacques. I thought I worked with right-minded people, who were as honest as me and who believed in the company and now…"

"You're not so sure," Jacques offered as the culmination of her thought.

"Maybe," she said quietly. She glanced over the piles of paper and printouts. "There's still a lot here to work through, Jacques, and I'm going to have to put it to one side until the beginning of next month."

"But I would suggest that a full audit of expenses is required, Michelle. Is there no way that we can do that?"

Michelle let out a deep sigh. "The only thing I can do is to offer some overtime this weekend to a couple of the admin staff—"

"No!" Jacques interrupted her. "I'm sorry," he added, taking in her startled expression. "I don't want anyone from Édouard's half of the organisation working on this at all."

"Oh, I see. You've no need to worry. Because HR work includes a lot of confidential and financial information, I have my own admin team who work only for me. The two people I'm talking about are engaged to each other and the extra money will help them."

"I see. Do they have the capability to undertake this kind of analysis?"

"No, not really, but I know they can be trusted, they are both dedicated employees and, with some coaching from me, they will do a good job for you."

"Alright. Set that up, please. Leave them my contact number for advice over the weekend and we'll talk again on Monday."

When Jacques finally arrived at the chalet, Beth was sitting on the floor of the snug surrounded by the contents of the boxes and files she had collected from Old Thierry.

"Bad day?"

Jacques dumped his bag on the settee and collapsed down beside it.

"That's one description." He unbuttoned his jacket and ran his hand through his hair.

"Should I keep guessing, or are you going to tell me about whatever is bothering you?"

"It's this investigation, Beth, and, no, I don't want to talk about it or the day I've had. So, why don't you tell me what all this is?" He sat forward and picked up a wallet of negatives and then a pile of black and white photographs and began to look through them.

"Well, I've had an idea...and I'd like to know if you think it's right or not?" She looked up at him and he shrugged as he waited for her to continue.

"You said it was Thierry's ninetieth birthday soon, didn't you?"

"Yes, it's at the end of December, I think, but Gaston and Marianne know the exact date because they are planning a surprise party for him."

"Well, I thought I would create a photographic tribute to Thierry in the form of a book and give it to him on his birthday. There are shots here that date from the thirties,

Jacques. What I have here is a pictorial history of Mende and the surrounding area. I want to put something together for Thierry and then, if he gives me his permission, to take it to an agent to see if there is a possible market for the book commercially. What do you think?"

Jacques looked at her and smiled. "That sounds like a lot of work to me. Does that mean that you are going to stay here until Christmas?"

"Yes, I think it does!"

surveillance camera footage

Hélène moves into view. "Serge, how are you?" She giggles and removes her cigarettes and matches from her coat pocket.

21/10/2009 16.33.48

Serge stays out of view. "Hélène, and I'm fine, thanks."
Her cigarette lit, she tosses the match into the ashcan. "So, how's everything with you?"

21/10/2009 16.34.07

"Fine."
"No security scares?"
There's no answer.

21/10/2009 16.34.19

Hélène takes a long drag on her cigarette before speaking. "And what about Luc? How's he?"
"If you really want to know that, why don't you ask him yourself?"

21/10/2009 16.34.31

Hélène puts her head on one side. "Now, Serge, it sounds to me like you're having a difficult day. Is there anything I can do to help?"

21/10/2009 16.34.48

"No, thanks."
The roller door moves up and Madeleine comes into view. "You wanted to talk, Hélène."

21/10/2009 16.34.57

Hélène nods. "You asked me for feedback about Aimée's presentation yesterday to all the department heads concerning the new internal communications strategy."

21/10/2009 16.35.12

"Go on."

"I thought her slides were well done, but the content was mediocre. There was only the minimum amount of information there with all the detail in the supporting notes."

21/10/2009 16.35.31

"She has a soft voice, Madeleine, so she comes across as far too timid for a Communications Manager. So, I think you should be recommending some coaching for her in that area."

21/10/2009 16.35.44

"When we got to the questions at the end she didn't sound convincing, especially when I asked her exactly how she would ensure that everyone complied with the new strategy. I don't think she's thought out—"

"Look, if you are going to discuss another member of staff like, this then you both need to be in a small meeting room upstairs by yourselves, not out here. It's not appropriate." Serge stubs out his cigarette.

21/10/2009 16.36.14

"And to make sure you get a balanced view, Madeleine, I was at that event also. I thought her slides and the notes were exactly what was required. I thought she handled the questions from all the staff very well," he added.

21/10/2009 16.36.29

"When you ambushed her with your question, Hélène, you made yourself look foolish. Aimée handled the situation with her usual courtesy and grace." Serge moves into view and keys in the entrance code on the key pad.

He looks straight at Hélène. "You need to learn discretion, Madame, and if anyone's behaviour needs to be discussed, it's both of yours."

Serge disappears out of view.

21/10/2009 16.36.57

thursday, october 22nd

Jacques' morning had begun well, and as he crossed the road to Vaux Consulting, he relished the thought of interviewing Édouard's PA. Whilst she hadn't been in the employ of the Vaux Group in 1971, she had been in the company a long time, and he thought that if anyone could unlock the mystery of the possible missing child it might be her.

Minutes later and, settled in her office, he took a sip of the coffee she had placed in front of him. "You've worked with Édouard for a long time, Mademoiselle Lapointe. You must get to know someone pretty well after, what is it, twenty-six years."

"I know how Édouard works, but I wouldn't say I know him well. I only see him and deal with him in a work context." Her face was perfectly composed as she looked directly at Jacques.

"Before you worked here, what did you do?" He retrieved his notebook from his jacket pocket and waited for her response.

"I was at university until I was twenty-three. Then I travelled for a while, eventually returning to France when I was twenty-five because my mother had become seriously ill. But I don't see the relevance of this to your investigation, Monsieur Forêt."

Jacques grinned. "The name is still Jacques! As for the investigation, I have a lot of suspects who all have means and opportunity but no apparent motive. I am now looking into the detail of everyone's background. At university until you were twenty-three – that seems late to me," he said as he jotted the information down.

"I did some travelling before attending university." Her hands resting one on top of the other in her lap, she still gave nothing away.

Jacques made a note and then underlined it. "When you began to work here, who was Édouard's previous personal assistant?"

"His current wife. She was pregnant with the twins and had decided to become a full-time mother to enable her to look after the children. I was recruited to fill her post on a permanent basis from the outset."

"What about Édouard's life before then? Do you know anything about that? For instance, when he first started the company?" Pen poised, he was eager to portray the idea that he knew nothing of the organisation's history.

"He didn't. It was his father's company. Monsieur Édouard is the eldest son and he came to work in the original company when he was twenty-one. His father needed some help – the business had already been expanding for a while – and Monsieur Vaux senior had plans to diversify further. Monsieur Alain joined the company about four years later. Not long after that, their father suffered a serious stroke and had to retire early, and the company was then re-organised, re-branded and registered as the Vaux Group with responsibilities assigned to each brother as they are now."

"And what about in 1971, Mademoiselle? Do you know or have you heard anything about what happened to Édouard in 1971?"

"I overheard him arguing with his brother as a result of your questioning him yesterday, but that's all."

"Hmm. And what about you, Mademoiselle? Where were you in 1971?"

"I was studying at the lycée, Monsieur, here in Mende."

Jacques quickly glanced at his notebook where he had noted her date of birth. *Sixteen in 1971.* An echo of Édouard's comments drifted through his mind and he made a note to cross-check Mademoiselle Lapointe's education in minute detail.

113

"Thank you, and just a few more questions. What are your connections with C and C Consulting?"

For the first time during the interview, Mademoiselle Lapointe looked away for a moment before replying. "I only come in contact with their employees as a direct result of work in support of Monsieur Édouard. I don't know any of their staff on a personal level. Naturally, I have met most of the directors on several occasions, and always in a work context, but that is all."

"And I suppose leaking information to them is something that you would never do?" He watched her face for any reaction at all.

"That's correct, Monsieur Forêt." She looked him in the eye. Her posture unchanging, her expression blank and her gaze steady and unfathomable.

Philippe Chauvin was on the phone when Jacques arrived in his office at the agreed time that afternoon.

"Come in, Jacques, and sit down. I'll just be a moment." Removing his hand from the mouthpiece, he continued his call. "Yes, and we need that spec by Monday," he said before pausing. "OK. Thanks." Philippe hung up and turned his attention to Jacques. "I understand you have some more questions for me about the network." He sat back and pushed his chair out from the desk. "Fire away."

"Our discussion the other evening has made me realise that there's still a lot more that I need to know and some questions that I neglected to ask because we ran out of time. One of the most important issues is for me to understand just how good our network security is."

"Our security is as good as we can get it, Jacques. We don't have a virtual private network, which would be more secure, because we cannot justify the cost of the installation and upgrade at this point. It is something that we have discussed at board meetings, and I'm confident, in a couple of years when we undertake the next scheduled technology refresh, that we will be in a position to upgrade to a VPN."

"Are you saying that, currently, it is easy for a hacker to

access our network at any time?"

Philippe smiled. "Not exactly. What I'm saying is that we are living with an acceptable and manageable level of vulnerability. Just look around you, Jacques. We have a substantial number of employees who are divided into groups and each group has discreet access to specific areas of the network. All of which is protected by individual passwords and logins. But, as much as we impress upon everyone not to share their login details, they do! Not logging out of a machine whilst away from their desk means that any visitor could access any of the documents on that person's machine. A really determined and skilful hacker could, with some relatively simple code on a data stick, copy key documents or specific files."

"I've looked at how we manage visitors to the building already, Philippe, and I've been through the records that we keep and compared those details with the list of visitors who have been given system access that you supplied. Overlaying that information with the details of who has had access to the tenders that have failed indicates to me that the threat is from inside the organisation. There is someone, or a small group of people, in one or both halves of the group who is involved in or responsible for these continued security leaks. Do you know of any way in which a company employee can access data that they shouldn't without detection?"

Philippe frowned. "That's quite an assumption, Jacques. Whether it was an outsider or someone on staff, they would have to be physically present in the building. Anyone could access the system by using known log-in details or using an open account. He or she would then be able to install a piece of software on a specific desktop PC which could then be set running to collect a set of data that would be channelled to an already identified account, for example, an email account or to a personal IP address. But we have inbuilt security protocols on the network and any such software would be detected by us."

"But if, as I now suspect, the individual is from within

the company and knows how those protocols work, would they be able to avoid them?"

"Are you suggesting that someone in my business area might be responsible?" Philippe pulled his chair closer to the desk. "Because if you are, you need to understand that I have personally vetted all of my key staff and I believe them all to be trustworthy." He sat forward, his hands linked on his desk.

"I'm not suggesting that. But I am now convinced that someone within Vaux is behind the losses and possibly the cyber-attack last week. I think that there may be other people outside of the group who are also involved, and I need to do some further work to find out if that assumption is true and who those people might be. My question, then: Is it possible to avoid the protocols?"

"In theory, yes, but in practice it would mean a high level of knowledge and it would be difficult to execute."

"But possible."

"Yes. Anything else, Jacques?"

"If you were to access our network to look at files that you were not authorised to access, how would you do it?"

Philippe raised his eyebrows and shook his head. "Am I your chief suspect?"

"No, but I need your expertise, Philippe, and I would like you to answer my question."

"OK, I would use the shared computer at our reception points in each building. They are the only shared computers on the network. We did have others, but when I arrived I made it a company policy to keep shared computers to a minimum. Those two PCs have a shared password that everyone on the security team knows. I would install some code and leave it to run, probably overnight or for a fixed period, to collect whatever data was required, for example, login details. Once I'd got that I could, as an illustration, change who has access to specific files, and then, from my own computer, I could login and take whatever data I required or get an accomplice to do it for me."

"And is all of that possible without leaving a trace on

system?"

"There is always a trace left on system, Jacques, always. Think about it. You work on a file and save it. The next time you open it, as it loads up it shows when it was last edited. Most people don't notice because they are busy and just want to get on with their work. But if that file had been accessed between you last saving it and you next working on it, it would be obvious and you could and should report it as a security breach. In reality, it never happens."

Jacques stared out of the window as he formed his next question. "So, if I were to give you a list of tender documents that Alain and myself believe have been leaked, could you undertake the same sort of audit trail that you did for the letter to Nicolas Durand?"

"Sure. But my team are still working on the fallout from the cyber-attack, so anything else will have to wait until we know what happened. Just get me the list, and we'll look at it as soon as we can."

"Thanks, I'll email that over." Jacques got up and paused. A question was lurking at the back of his mind but he wasn't quite sure exactly what it was he wanted to know, and he couldn't seem to encourage his mind to let the question move into his conscious.

"Is there something else, Jacques?" Philippe was about to head for the door.

"I'm not sure, but if it is possible to access the network and install software to collect data, then it must also be possible to copy everything any one person does on their PC?"

"Subject to gaining access to the actual PC, yes." Philippe smiled and led the way out of the room.

"And what about the cyber-attack?"

"Still not resolved, as I said, but we have found some spurious code and we are examining that now. We're still not entirely sure how they got past our security but I will let you know what we find."

Jacques left Philippe and took the stairs to return to his own office.

In Paris, a plane touched down and taxied to its terminal in the dullness of a late grey afternoon. As soon as he saw the lighted instruction to remove his seatbelt, Richard Laurent Delacroix unbuckled his and stood. The six-and-a-half-hour non-stop flight from Québec City was about as much as he could tolerate.

Unlike his father and uncle, he was tall, broad-shouldered and muscled. There was also a swank about him that had definitely got one of the air hostesses interested, and he fully intended to make the most of the opportunity. He had planned a forty-eight hour stop-over in Paris, but that could be extended. He could catch the shuttle to Le Puy-en-Velay on Monday or Tuesday and re-scheduling would just be the price of the administration fee. The last place he really wanted to be was in some backwater of a village sitting half way up a mountain.

He smoothed his thick silver grey hair back and opened the locker above his seat. He always travelled light, a single suitcase in the hold and his carry-on luggage was one small case, his black winter coat and a matching fedora.

"My card," he said to the blonde air hostess. "I'm in Paris by myself for the weekend. Call me anytime." Then he gave her his well-practiced winning smile and a flash of his sparkling blue eyes and stepped off the plane.

Immigration and luggage retrieval took almost an hour but, once out on the concourse, he was able to get a taxi straight away. It took two attempts for the driver to understand his Canadian French request to take him to his hotel in Opéra, the 9th *arrondissement*. The ensuing conversation with the driver was stilted and Ricky had to remind himself that claiming Québécois ancestry wouldn't work when he finally arrived in his uncle's village of Messandrierre. They would know that his ancestry only stretched as far back as his father rather than the original settlers from the seventeenth century. But the lie worked well with clients, and he had no intention of abandoning it permanently. He recognised he would just need to be careful for the next few weeks or however long it would take to sort out his uncle's estate. Not that he was expecting great things. But a farm meant land and land meant cash – his sole interest. And there was that name, Messandrierre. He made a mental note to ensure he got the pronunciation just right, and just French.

***

The bar in the village was noisy and full following the *Maire*'s municipality meeting. Gaston and Marianne were busy with orders for drinks.

Jacques, sat at a table by the window, pushed his chair a little further back and took a slug of beer from his glass.

"Fermier Pamier, how is business going for you?"

"Well, I'm away a lot at the moment, but business is good, Jacques." The farmer looked around the room.

"And Madame Pamier…how is she coping with you being away so much?" Jacques remained relaxed but he watched the farmer closely.

Pamier shrugged. "She knows the cattle; she knows what she's doing."

"And she's not finding it difficult without the help you used to have?"

Pamier thumped his almost empty beer glass on the table. "What's that supposed to mean?" His weathered round cheeks flushed and he glared at Jacques.

"Juan de Silva, the help you used to have. What happened to him?"

Pamier looked away.

"We questioned your wife about his disappearance a few months ago. Did she tell you?"

Pamier remained silent.

"You were away at the time, I seem to remember." Jacques still waited for a response, but Pamier looked into his beer glass and drained the last few drops.

"You see, we have some new information." The farmer

looked straight at him. Jacques felt Pamier's eyes boring into him.

"You're no longer on the force, Monsieur Forêt." He stood and pushed his chair back under the table with a sharp grating noise on the tiled floor. "I don't have to answer your questions because you are not a policeman and this is not an official police enquiry."

"I can soon make it one!" Jacques stood and moved to block Pamier's path. "Gendarme Clergue is just over there," he said shifting his gaze towards the corner of the bar and nodding. "We can invite him over here and make this conversation official."

"What new evidence?" Pamier stood his ground.

"A letter from his family containing some interesting information they have been given by someone who knew Juan."

Pamier stared at him and then, taking a step back, he let out a dry, hollow laugh. "You're bluffing," he said and moved quickly to the other side of the bar.

Jacques re-positioned his chair so that he could watch the whole of the room. Pamier ordered another beer and then leaned against the counter waiting. A few moments later, he and Gaston were in conversation, and shortly after that they both went into the small office at the far corner of the room.

Fermier Rouselle got up and began collecting the empty glasses from the table.

"What's happening about the compensation for your cattle, Rouselle?" asked one of the three other men drinking at his table

"Nothing!" Retorted Rouselle. "It's red tape. It could take months." He made a move towards the bar and then stopped and turned to his companions. "But you know what, I'm looking after Delacroix's herd until his nephew arrives and when he does, he might just find that it's two less than he thought!" He let out a forced roar of a laugh and made his way to the bar to give Marianne an order for the round of drinks.

"Ah Rouselle, even Canadians can count, you know."

The three other men erupted into laughter.

"He's Québécois!" shouted Rouselle from the bar. "He's a city man! What does he know?" After a short conversation with Marianne, Rouselle carried three beers back to the table and left them. Returning to the bar, he picked up his own glass, took a gulp and walked over to Gaston's office, entered and closed the door behind him.

Jacques picked up his empty glass and joined Clergue and the *Maire* at the bar.

"Another beer, Jacques?" The *Maire* was already beckoning Marianne across to him before Jacques could answer and whether he wanted one or not, a clean glass was filled and placed on a mat in front of him.

"I've just rattled Pamier," he said in a low voice. "He's in the office with Gaston and Rouselle."

"Gaston?" Clergue folded his arms across his chest. "Gaston can't possibly have anything to do with de Silva's disappearance, can he?"

"I hope not," said Jacques, "but you may want to follow up with some enquiries of your own in a couple of days. Pamier thinks we've got new evidence."

"Is that true?"

Jacques shook his head.

The *Maire* raised an eyebrow. "I didn't hear that last comment, Jacques." He took his whisky and gently set it swirling around the bottom of the glass. "The lumber for the new fencing around the campsite will be arriving tomorrow. Gaston is going to need some help to get the fencing erected over the next week. If you both could lend a hand I would appreciate it." He looked from one to other.

"I have some time on Saturday," said Jacques, "but I expect Gaston will need both of us on Sunday, Thibault, as he and Marianne will be busy in the restaurant." A nod from each sealed the deal.

friday, october 23rd, 2.25am

Fermier Rouselle drove his tractor across his north pasture to the corner of the field that butted up against Delacroix's land and the boundary of a now long-abandoned farm that sat at the far eastern edge of the village. In the head lights, he could see the dark figures of Gaston and Fermier Pamier by the large pine tree at the corner of the pasture. He stopped the tractor and cut the engine. From the trailer at the back, he brought out spades, wiring, stakes, a hammer and Tilley lamps.

"Right, what Delacroix's nephew doesn't know about is only my business," he said. "I want this boundary back where it should be and where it is on my deeds, and that's a metre and half down this slope." He dropped the coil of wire and returned to bring the stakes.

Gaston stubbed out his cigarette. "It's going to be obvious what we've done, Rouselle, in daylight. Anyone who comes up here regularly will see what we've done straight away."

Rouselle attacked the rickety fencing already in place and pulled it out of the ground in seconds. "I want my land back," he shouted, "and I'm going to get it before that nephew arrives and interferes."

Gaston and Pamier exchanged a glance. "And you're sure it's a metre and a half down the slope?"

Rouselle hefted a stake into place by the tree and began hammering it into the earth. "I'm certain." The stake steady, he dropped his hammer into a pocket of his overalls and took one and a half strides. "To here and up there in a straight line; this side of that outcrop of boulders to the corner of my fencing. My land." The farmer picked up

122

another stake and set to work.

"You get the wire, and I'll dismantle the rest of Delacroix's old fence," said Pamier. "We'll stay well back."

Gaston moved the coil of wire and began attaching it to the first stake. "I don't like this."

"Be quiet and let Rouselle get ahead. And whatever happens, keep your mouth shut. I don't think we have anything to fear. Just get on with the work and stay well back. OK?"

The three men worked on in almost complete silence for the next hour. The sky was clear and the moon bright. The Tilley lamps only required to provide a little supplementary lighting when Rouselle was digging holes for the stakes to be slotted into.

Rouselle was right below the boulders. Stabbing his spade into the ground, he felt it slice through the gelatinousness of what he thought felt like peat, only to feel the tool come up against something akin to the friable hardness of limestone. It stopped him dead. He called to Pamier for extra light. Gaston remained where he was.

Under the light from the Tilley lamp, Rouselle scraped the topsoil away by hand, and recoiled at what he had unearthed. "We need Jacques," he shouted after stepping a few paces back. "Phone him and get him up here right now."

***

"I want an explanation, and none of you are leaving here until I get one." Jacques, unshaven from having being woken so early, and dressed in a pair of creased jeans and a jumper, paced back and forth in the bar as he waited for someone to respond. "This find has to be called in. There is no question of that. But you will have to explain what you were doing up in the north pastures at four in the morning. It's a very odd time to be mending fences, Rouselle." His tone hardened. "What were you doing?" He stopped and looked each one of the men in the eye in turn. "Rouselle?"

123

he prompted.

Rouselle shifted in his chair and looked away. Gaston and Pamier glanced at each other but said nothing.

"Right." Jacques pulled out his phone. "You leave me no option, and the charges I will be suggesting to my old colleagues in Mende will be trespass, concealment of a body and obstruction of a police investigation. I'm sure I can think of a couple more, but those will suffice for now." He began to dial.

"Tell him, Rouselle." It was Gaston who broke the silence. "Damn well tell him, man."

Jacques pulled up a chair from a nearby table, pulled his notebook from the back pocket of his jeans and sat down. "Any chance of some coffee?"

"Of course," said Gaston. He got up and moved behind the bar.

"It's not trespass, Jacques." Rouselle blustered. "I was taking back what was mine." He sat upright, his hands placed on his thighs, defiance in his eyes. "I was taking back my land."

"And do you have documentary proof of where the boundary between your land and Delacroix's actually sits?"

"Yes!"

"So, if I was to ask for those documents so that I could pass them on to a surveyor, he will be able to tell me that your new fence is in exactly the right place. Is that correct?" Jacques watched the farmer's face as a smidgen of colour suffused his cheeks.

"I'm just a simple farming man, Jacques," he said, his tone more moderate and respectful. "I understand cattle and the land. How do I know what a surveyor will find?" He shrugged off his evident lie.

Jacques tapped his notebook with his pen. "And why did this…reclaim of your land have to be undertaken now? It's 4.37am; it's still dark. Moving fences is not the sort of job that I would normally expect to be done at this time in the morning." He accepted the coffee that Gaston handed to him and sat back in his chair, left ankle resting on his knee.

124

"I've a very busy day today and I wanted to get the job done and out of the way early." Rouselle placed the coffee he was handed on the table next to him.

"I see. You have such a busy day today that you can afford to keep lying to me, can you? No-one is leaving until I get to the truth, Fermier Rouselle. The whole truth."

"Delacroix owes me," he shouted. "And I'm not giving up on my land. I'm doing my bit for the community by taking care of his cattle, as requested by Monsieur le Maire, even though the compensation for those two beasts of mine that he injured and Clergue killed is still outstanding. I want my land back." He stared at Jacques.

"Then do it legally, Rouselle. And after the funeral. What you've been doing here tonight is disrespectful and highly suspicious. I have no doubt that your new fence will be more or less in the right place, Fermier Rouselle. But, more or less is still not exact and still not legal."

Before the farmer could remonstrate more, he turned his attention to Gaston. "And your involvement is what?"

"I was just helping out a fellow villager, that's all, Jacques." Gaston finished his coffee and took out his cigarettes and lighter.

"Fermier Pamier, your reason for being there?"

"The same as Gaston." The both exchanged a look.

Jacques drained his cup and placed it on the table behind him. "And what about the body. Do any of you know who it is?"

"No," the three of them chorused.

"Is that so?" Jacques stood and began to pace, his instincts sharpened by their response.

"So, none of you knew the body was there before you found it?"

"No." Another unified response.

"You don't seem very surprised that there is a body on what you claim to be your land, Fermier Rouselle?"

Rouselle opened his mouth to speak but paused and closed it again.

"Nothing to say, Fermier Rouselle?" Jacques waited.

"That's not like you, is it? Always voluble. Always to be relied upon for an appropriate opinion. But today, when a body is found on your land, you say nothing."

Rouselle stood. "And you're not a gendarme any longer, this isn't Paris, and you have no right to interrogate me."

Jacques turned to face him and shouted. "That may be so, but you sent for me, so sit down. You've involved me in this very suspicious escapade that you three are undertaking and I have to be absolutely certain that I am not implicated in any way. My reputation as a gendarme and investigator is at stake and you three seem to think that you can just brush that aside behind a wall of silence." Hands on his hips he towered over them. "I'm calling this in, I expect it will be Magistrate Pelletier who is assigned to this enquiry and I expect the three of you to be absolutely open and honest with him as you seem to be incapable of being truthful with me."

Leaving his notebook on the table, he marched out of the bar, phone in his hand, and dialled.

"The body has been removed and I've left the crime scene officers to do their job. It looks as though he was in the ground for some time." Pelletier followed Jacques through to the kitchen of Beth's chalet.

"Any evidence of cause of death?" Jacques spooned coffee into the pot and set it on the hob.

"Gunshot wound to the side of the face. Identification may be a little difficult." Pelletier took the stool indicated and sat down.

"Murder, then. A contract killing, do you think? The Devereux clan from Marseille still have connections in Mende and St-Etienne."

Pelletier shook his head. "I doubt it. Contract killers would make a better job of obliterating any identifying features and would remove the hands too. If he exists on the database, we may find him from his fingerprints."

"But you're not hopeful?"

"No. From his clothes I'd say he was a casual labourer,

possibly a traveller. I'll await the pathologist's report. For now, I just need to know what you can tell me about all of this."

Jacques poured the coffee and took the stool opposite Pelletier. He opened his notebook and read the details.

"I was called to the scene at 3.36am. Gaston phoned me. I took the bike and arrived at the scene at 3.57am. I secured the scene as quickly as I could and escorted the three of them to the bar and questioned them. Their stated reason for being in the north pasture was so that Rouselle could reclaim land that Fermier Guy Delacroix had taken." He looked up at the Magistrate, discarded his notebook and sighed. "This argument between Delacroix and Rouselle has been going on for years. When I was gendarme here it would flare up every couple of months. Delacroix died recently, and I think Rouselle saw his opportunity to resolve the boundary issue before Delacroix's only relative arrives from Canada. I told Rouselle to deal with the issue legally and respectfully. Delacroix isn't even in the ground yet!"

Pelletier took off his spectacles and began to clean them on his handkerchief. "And what about the body?"

"I couldn't get anything out of them. But they know more than they are saying. When I asked them if they knew who the person might have been they hid behind silence. I am certain that in the time between my being called and arriving at the scene they made some sort of agreement amongst themselves."

"I think you're right. I've questioned them individually, and they are all responding in exactly the same way. Who do we lean on?" Pelletier replaced his spectacles and stared at his coffee.

"Gaston. He's got a record. It's from a long time ago but it's there and you can use it as a lever. You might also want to remind him that there have been occasions when he has taken too hard a line with visitors to the campsite which I've had to smooth over. He doesn't need to know you've got that from me because news travels fast and extensively in this village, but he won't be pleased if you do remind

127

him."

"And if he doesn't crack? Who's next?"

Jacques thought for a moment. "I think Gaston will give, but if not then try Rouselle. He blusters a lot and likes to shout and demand his rights, but essentially, he's an honest man. Whilst I was questioning them in the bar I noticed Gaston and Pamier exchanging glances. Those two are colluding about something, I'm sure of it."

Pelletier picked up his coffee and drank. "Any unsolved cases, Jacques?"

"Everything on my desk before I left the service was resolved apart from the disappearance of Juan de Silva. I am also aware that Gendarme Clergue has had some recent correspondence from the family in Spain and has been asking questions in the village. But nothing new has come of it. And Pamier is also implicated in that case."

"Ahh. Interesting. We'll get a positive identification first." Pelletier pushed his half-drunk coffee away. "I'll need a formal statement from you when you're next in Mende."

"I'll come in first thing on Monday."

Pelletier nodded. "How's Beth?"

"She's well, thank you, and has been making plans for some sort of future here in France." He smiled.

"She's decided to stay?" Pelletier stood and put his notebook in his coat pocket.

"It's a very difficult decision for her and she is still working it through. She has to make her own choice, Bruno, and I'm being patient. However long it takes, I will be patient. But, she told me yesterday that she was thinking about opening a photographic studio in Mende. Apparently, it was something that Old Thierry, an elderly photographer whose been here in the village for many years, suggested to her a couple of days ago. That's where she is this afternoon, making enquiries with an estate agent."

"And you? How do you feel about that?"

"I couldn't be happier."

The last of the properties was the one that had especially captured Beth's interest. It was the place that Old Thierry had once used when he worked full time and had a family to support. It was just off the Boulevard du Soubeyran, and in the twenty years since the old man had last been a tenant it had been a hairdresser's, a mobile-phone outlet, and a stationary shop with lengthy periods in between of vacancy.

Beth stood opposite the front of the property and consulted the papers the Estate Agent had given her. *Hmm, good frontage.* She moved across the narrow street and peered in through the window.

"This would easily take a large display. A wedding photo, maybe. No. I know: a scenic display to create a background. Then here, towards the front, a wedding photo with a low table or display unit laid with a small bouquet and a wedding album. Hmm." She took a couple of steps back and knocked into a tall, thin man in a dark green hoodie.

"I'm so sorry," she said and stepped closer to the window.

The man just grunted and moved on swiftly. Beth looked down the street after him. *Some people have no manners!* Checking the immediate space around her was clear on both sides, she moved back again and considered the interior. The short counter at the back would be sufficient for taking telephone calls and handling payments. *But what about the walls? Some displays for cards, I think, just like the shop at home. Over there…some pictures and a display unit to hold framed and unframed prints, perhaps.* Then she thought about all the old cameras and lenses she had collected from Old Thierry on Tuesday. *I'd need some sort of shelving that is just out of reach and I could create a display. The old box camera could go up there, the 35mm…the three lenses…* In her mind's eye, she had furnished the space completely.

She glanced down at the sheets in her hand and re-read the details.

"And yes, as Thierry said, the back room is still available too." Mounting the single step, she pressed her nose against the glass panel of the door and tried to see through the glass of the closed connecting door into the second room, but there was just an impenetrable greyness.

Turning around, she looked at the properties across from where she was stood. *A café, that's good, there will be plenty of people passing by. A patisserie…mmm, all those cakes mean lots more people in the vicinity. That's got to be good. And a small boutique, even better, lots of young women around who may need a wedding photographer. Even better!*

"Thierry was right about that too. This is an excellent location." She checked the paperwork for the third time. "I need to do some maths," she said and folded the papers, put them back in her bag and made her way back to the Estate Agent's Office.

***

Hidden in the shadows a few doors down from where she had been standing, Luciole pulled at his green hoodie, hitched his rucksack further up his shoulder and moved back onto the street. He'd recognised her instantly as the woman at the hunting lodge he'd been watching on Tuesday. He had nothing else to do and now, he was curious. Thinking there might be a useful opportunity, he followed her at a distance and frequently moved from one side of the street to the other and back again.

When she went into the Estate Agents' office he continued on a few metres, crossed the street, and hid in a small alley and waited. When she re-emerged, she was with another woman and they were talking. He followed them back to the property and this time they went inside. He went into the café opposite and, after ordering, took a seat by the window. The woman behind the counter was watching him. He took off his hoodie and leered at her. She looked away and got on with her work.

About an hour later the two women came back out onto the street, talked for a few moments and then shook hands. The woman he'd seen at the chalet went left down the street towards the Tourist Information Office, the other woman went in the opposite direction.

Luciole pulled out his phone and switched it on.

That job. Easy. Next week. Know where. Meet me. Need money. Luc

His text sent, he pocketed the phone, gathered his hoodie and rucksack together and left, a wide grin on his face.

monday, october 26th

"Sorry, I'm a little late, Michelle." Jacques breezed in to the small meeting room on the floor below his own office at the Vaux Investigations building. "I had to call into the gendarmerie this morning and my business there took a little longer than expected." He threw his coat over the back of one of the chairs and settled himself in another. "So, what have you got for me?"

"It's not good. The claiming in advance and the drawing of money from cash machines on the company credit cards is endemic within one team. All the senior managers and some of their immediate sub-ordinates are working their expenses in the same way. We've also discovered that the credit cards are being shared between some senior managers and their more junior staff."

Michelle produced a file and pushed it across the table. "In there you'll find a link and a password to a folder that we've created with all the electronic copies of the papers we've examined. There is also a file in that folder that lists the names of those we believe may be involved."

Jacques flipped open the cover of the file and leafed through the first couple of pages. "Which team?"

"The principle project team that works directly to Édouard."

"So, that's Madeleine Cloutier and her people?"

Michelle nodded.

"And which directors?

"All of them except Roger Baudin, the HR Director, and Philippe Chauvin."

Jacques raised an eyebrow, "In other words all the directors who work directly to Édouard. It's good to know that Roger is honest as he manages all of the group's finances and…" Jacques stared past Michelle as a realisation came into his mind.

"Roger Baudin's mobile phone records. I've been looking at those over the last week and we only have call histories for two phones."

"Yes, that's right, his personal phone that he sometimes uses for business calls over the weekend or in the evenings and his office phone. But he always itemises everything exactly, even the occasional personal call on his business phone, for which he never claims."

"I see. So why does he need a third phone?" Jacques stared straight ahead. "Why would you want a third phone?"

"Jacques? Are you asking me that question or just—"

"Sorry, I was thinking out loud. It's nothing, and thank you for all the work you and your team have done here," he said taking the file and putting it in his bag.

"Jacques, how are you going to use this information? I mean…are you going to take it to the police?"

"I'm not sure yet. But if there is any kind of petty theft within the Vaux Group, it needs to be identified and dealt with, and Alain and Édouard will make the final decision on what action is to be taken. My current investigation has stalled. Someone is, or some people are, lying. Having this information means that I may be able to apply some pressure to help me break the deadlock." He picked up his coat.

"There's one more thing. Madeleine Cloutier claims expenses for a meeting in Rodez every Friday. A couple of months ago, I asked her why and she told me to mind my own business. The thing is, the project that the meeting was to support was finalised fourteen months ago. It's true we do provide support following the completion of our contracted input but that is usually only for about three months. I made a couple of phone calls to the previous client and it appears she has not been to see them since her last contracted visit in January. The other thing you need to know is that there is a large branch of C and C Consulting in the centre of Rodez."

"Which means she is either going to see C and C, or someone else in Rodez, or she is going somewhere completely different for some reason. Have you challenged her again?"

Michelle shook her head. "I've just left it. When I asked her about the claim before she became very aggressive. She accused me of interfering and questioning her integrity and she practically physically threw me out of her office."

Jacques smiled. "Leave it with me."

"Hélène, I wanted to ask you some more detailed questions concerning the letter that was sent to Nicolas Durand."

"We've already talked about this, Jacques, and I told you I didn't recognise it." She crossed her legs, wrapped her linked hands around her knee and smiled.

"Yes, but I've had the IT team do some checking for me. They have an audit trail that puts the original letter in a folder on the network that you access and that clearly shows that you altered the text of the file." He placed in front of her a printout showing the path and her name against the changes made to the file.

"As I said, Jacques, I don't remember the letter and anyone could have used my computer when I wasn't there. I'm always forgetting to log out." She shrugged and grinned.

"So, you are openly admitting that you have shared your log-in details and password with other people, which is against company policy. How many people have that information, Hélène?"

"That's not what I—"

"You said," he interrupted, his tone hard and commanding, "that anyone could have used your computer. But in order to access that particular folder they would have to have your password and log-in. How widely have you shared those details?"

Hélène stared through narrowed eyelids but said nothing.

Jacques let the strained silence fester. He remained still and determined, watching his interviewee as a hawk eyes its prey.

"I haven't shared my log-in or password," she said in a harsh whisper.

"So, you're now admitting that you changed the letter, are you? Because if you are, then I want to know what else you have told me that isn't true?"

Hélène raised her hand. "No, that is not what I'm saying. I don't remember the letter and I haven't shared my log-in. I don't know who changed that letter or how they did it."

Jacques nodded and turned to a different page in his notebook. "On your application for your job here at Vaux Consulting you said you had previously worked in Orléans and that you resigned that post after 18 months." He looked up from his notes to see that she had a fixed smile on her face. She gave him the smallest of nods of agreement.

"But it's not actually true, is it, Hélène? Do you want to tell me what really happened?"

She pushed her spectacles up to the bridge of her nose. "I didn't get on very well with my boss and we agreed that perhaps I should look for another job."

"That's an interesting interpretation." He consulted his notes. "According to the information I've received from that employer's HR manager, you were sacked after eight-and-a-half months. Can you tell me why?"

"I don't see what this has got to do with you or your work?"

"I'll remind you, shall I?" Jacques pulled out a lengthy letter on which he had highlighted certain phrases and paragraphs. "In Orléans, you were pulled up about your conduct in front of a senior manager on a number of occasions which resulted in an informal warning. You received a formal warning about your time-keeping, your high absences because of illness, and for taking time off without explanation. You received a further formal warning because of a series of system security breaches. Two weeks later you went out for lunch, came back drunk and, when

135

prevented from entering the building by a security guard, you became aggressive and abusive. The security guard made a formal complaint. You were then formally disciplined for being drunk during working hours and asked to leave. You did not respond by the due date and your contract was terminated." Jacques looked up. "What else have you re-invented or re-interpreted, Hélène?"

She played with the hair at the back of her neck and turned away.

"Alright. Let's look at your time in Rouen, shall we? Your employer there was most accommodating and sent me copies of various documents, including your application for the post they eventually awarded to you."

Jacques pulled out a photocopy and presented it to her. "This section here," he said pointing to the top of the second page, "is how you recorded your previous employment record then. This shows that you were unemployed at the time of completion of the form and that you were out of the country prior to that."

"That was true," she snapped. "I was in Belgium."

Jacques smirked. "For two years? Are you sure about that? I can't help noticing that the period you have put on this application covers your spell of employment in Orléans and your period of unemployment. Making false declarations seems to be commonplace to you."

Hélène stood. "I don't have to listen to anymore of—"

"Yes, you do." Jacques was on his feet and at the door barring her exit before she had had time to take a step. "SIT DOWN!"

Hélène's face blanched at the fierceness of his tone as she backed away and, after a moment's hesitation, resumed her seat.

"Your connections with C and C Consulting, is there anything new that you want to tell me, or anything that you've said previously that you want to change?"

"No."

"And you're absolutely certain about that?"

"Yes."

Jacques shook his head in disbelief, collected his papers together and left the room. He walked quickly along the corridor and ducked into a small store room and hid behind the door which he held ajar. A few moments later, he heard footsteps and Hélène walked by as she spoke into her phone. Once she had passed by, Jacques moved quietly out into the corridor and listened until she exited onto the stairwell. He had heard enough and he noted the time on the envelope from Rouen and drew a ring around it.

That conversation on the surveillance camera footage should be very interesting!

As he moved out onto the landing, his phone rang. It was Magistrate Bruno Pelletier, and he was required at the gendarmerie.

"We have a positive ID on the body from the north pasture above Messandrierre," said Pelletier as Jacques unbuttoned his coat and sat down.

"I don't think I need to ask, but I will. Who is it?"

"Juan de Silva. I'll need any information that you have, Jacques, before I go and question Pamier and the others."

Jacques nodded. "And do we have a detailed pathologist's report?"

"It was a12 bore shotgun wound, and it killed him outright."

"There's nothing more I can add to what I told you on Friday. Gendarme Clergue has all the papers, and if you need any help let me know."

"Will your plans for tomorrow morning enable you to be in the village at ten so that we can question Gaston, Pamier and Rouselle together?"

"Yes, I'll be there."

"And as you suggested, we'll start with Gaston."

***

The shuttle from Paris landed at Le Puy-en-Velay on time. Richard Delacroix cleared the airport, collected his hire car and took the RN88 to Messandrierre, arriving about an hour later. He parked in front of the bar and walked in.

"I'm looking for somewhere to stay," he said to the woman who was setting tables.

"I'm sorry, we don't have rooms. But there are some hunting lodges that you can rent. How long are you intending to stay?" Marianne placed the final piece of cutlery on the table and gave the stranger her full attention.

Richard flashed her his smile. "I'm not sure at the moment. The name's Richard Delacroix, but everyone calls me Ricky," he said proffering his hand. "I'm here for my uncle's funeral on Wednesday. I just need a place for a couple of days until I can get access to the house."

Marianne shook his hand briefly and took a step back. "I'm sorry for your loss, Monsieur Delacroix. If you will give me a moment, I'll check which of the chalets is free."

Ricky moved over to the bar and took in the whole room. "Just as I thought, some backwater of a place half way up a mountain." He turned and scanned the shelves of spirits. "Not even a decent bourbon to drink."

Marianne returned with a key fob and the receipt book. "Chalet number six is available until ten on Friday morning. We have a hunting party who are arriving that afternoon and all of the chalets are booked. I'm afraid that you will have to make other arrangements for Friday evening if you are still here."

"No problem. I fully expect to have access to my uncle's property by then. Which one is it?" He looked out of the windows and could only see the rise of ground and steps leading up to the camping area.

"You can't see it from here. Just take the road out of the car park on your right and follow it round. The first three chalets on your left are privately owned. Chalet six is on the right and between the camping area and the fork in the road. If you continue past it and take the right fork, you will see a dead oak tree on your left and your uncle's farm is immediately after that on your right."

"Right. I've got that."

Marianne took his details for her records and completed the receipt for the payment and handed over the key.

Ricky left and once back in his car followed the road as instructed. He didn't stop at the chalet but went straight on to find the farmhouse. He pulled up on the top road and got out and looked around. "My God, this place is desolate!" He took a few strides towards his new inheritance. The slippery mud stopped him and he looked with disdain at his soiled shoes. "Another time, I think." He inspected the property from where he was. "That looks no better than a wood shack! And I'm probably wasting my time." He returned to his car.

***

"Thanks, Gaston," Jacques put the newspaper to one side and picked up his beer. "The body you found has been positively identified." He replaced his glass on the white paper coaster and waited in vain for Gaston's reaction. "Aren't you curious to know who it is?" Jacques turned his glass, quarter turn by quarter turn expecting Gaston to respond. "You don't seem surprised or even interested, Gaston. Is that because you already know who it is?"

Gaston threw his cloth in the sink. "Alright, yes, I know who it is."

Jacques got up and, picking up the bunch of keys that Gaston had left on the bar, he went to the main door and locked it. "We need to talk. Magistrate Pelletier is coming here tomorrow morning and he will want answers, Gaston, so you'd better be prepared."

"I haven't done anything illegal, Jacques."

"Hiding a body is illegal, Gaston, last time I checked!" He slammed the keys on the bar.

Gaston smoothed his moustache, and then took out a cigarette and lit it. "It was the day I invited you to join the hunting party."

"That was two years-ago. November, and I'd not been here very long."

"And you were recovering from the gunshot wound you acquired in Paris."

Jacques grabbed his left shoulder and articulated the joint. "I wasn't in a very good frame of mind then."

"Too right!" Gaston flicked the ash from his cigarette into a small dish he kept behind the bar for when he had the place to himself. "You were a mess, and as I remember it at the first volley of shots you hit the ground, rolled and hit a boulder with your left shoulder. You were in a lot of pain. It was me who drove you to the hospital in Mende and brought you back here late that afternoon."

Jacques swallowed back the two years of feelings and emotions that he had consciously kept penned in the furthest reaches of his mind. He perched on the edge of a table to steady himself.

"You shouldn't have been left alone, but you insisted that I just help you into the house and then you sent me away." Gaston stubbed out his cigarette. "And when I came to check on you the next day you were still unconscious from the half bottle of whisky that you'd drunk and the painkillers you'd taken. You were a mess, man. You could have killed yourself!"

Jacques hadn't the energy to respond.

"After I'd dropped you off at your place on the day of the shoot, I saw Pamier running down the hill as I was driving away from the gendarmerie. He flagged me down and said he needed some help but he didn't say what. He got in the car, and it was only when we got back to the shoot that I saw what had happened. It was Pamier's idea to bury the body and say nothing. I tried to convince him to involve you but he wouldn't listen, and when I thought about the pain that you were in from the fall, I wasn't sure you could've handled it anyway. So I tried to persuade Pamier to leave the body where they found it until the following day, because I thought you might be able to handle the situation better. But, as it turned out, you were even less capable the next day."

Jacques took a deep breath. "Just be honest with Pelletier

tomorrow, and he doesn't need to know the detail about me that day or the next."

***

In the narrow streets of the oldest part of Mende, Luciole moved between the midnight shadows. From Boulevard de Soubeyran he took the side street and went to the shop that he'd seen Beth looking over. He looked through the windows. *Good. Still empty.*

He made his way to the back of the property. *It's left here and then left again into the courtyard. Wait! Someone might be watching... Nothing. No lights. No sound.* He stood in the small courtyard and looked around. *Narrow streets are perfect. I like narrow streets. Tall buildings. I can change them. I can destroy them.*

He identified the building he wanted and silently moved over towards it. *Four stories, linked attics probably. Old building with lots of old wood.* He stood back and looked at the open shutters on the single ground floor window. *Peeling paint... These shutters haven't been used for years.* He smiled as he thought about how he was going to make it burn.

Back on the main street, he pulled out his phone and sent a text.

Jobs a piece of piss Need box of crisps Need more money Luciole

tuesday, october 27th, 1.37am

The strangled wail as Jacques woke up from his dream terrified Beth. Her heart was pounding against her chest wall as she clutched at the duvet and sat bolt upright.

"Jacques, it's alright." She reached out to him. His skin was clammy and his breathing irregular and laboured. He sat forward, his arms resting on his raised knees.

"It's alright," she repeated as she stroked her hand down his arm.

He flinched at her touch. "I just need a few moments… Go back to sleep."

"No, Jacques, you need to talk about this. You need to tell me what this is all about and if I can help, I will."

He leaned back against the headboard and closed his eyes for a moment and let his breathing return to normal. "It's not good, Beth. These dreams are always about the last case I worked on in Paris, and what happened yesterday with Gaston in the bar has just brought it all to the front of my mind. I thought I was able to handle it… Maybe you're right."

Beth pulled the duvet around them both. "I'm listening."

"It was a case involving drugs. We were trying to get the supplier but he kept slipping through our fingers. He always seemed to be one step ahead. I was working undercover with another officer, you don't need to know who he was, but his assumed name was Khalid. He was of Moroccan descent and he could fit in well with the people we were investigating. It was Khalid who vouched for me with the drugs pushers when I joined the investigation team."

He pinched the bridge of his nose. "It was our last chance to get the supplier. He'd come to Paris and he'd got

142

shipments arriving from different locations into the city in a single 24-hour period. We knew exactly where to be and when, but about an hour before we were due to hit the warehouse, Khalid said the venue had changed. He said we had go to a building in Porte de la Villette in the 19th. We got there with about five minutes in which to get in place in readiness for the swoop on the much smaller building. We got the command to go in. Khalid went ahead and I followed with other officers entering from the back. The supplier and his men came out firing. I was assigned to take down the supplier. In the mêlée, he got past me. Khalid shouted and indicated the direction he wanted me to take and I followed the supplier out onto the street. I tackled him face down onto the pavement and when I turned him over to check it was the right man, I hesitated."

"Why?"

"Khalid had shouted something inside the warehouse and I hesitated because I realised that he'd used the wrong code word. He'd warned the supplier! Then the shot rang out and I hit the cobbles."

Jacques rolled his left shoulder over and a wave of pain moved through him. "That split second of thought is one of my worst mistakes and I still haven't forgiven myself for my stupidity."

"You have to let it go, Jacques."

"I don't know if I can. We got some arrests but we didn't get the supplier. There was an internal enquiry, but Khalid lied. He said he thought he was aiming at the supplier. He said he couldn't see my face. When he was questioned about the use of the wrong code word, he denied it. But I know what I heard. For a long time afterwards, I questioned my own memory and I doubted myself. But every time I went through what happened an image kept coming into my mind of Khalid holding his gun and pointing it directly at me."

"And yesterday in the bar with Gaston? What happened then?"

Jacques put his arm around her and she nestled her head

143

into the crook of his right shoulder. "I wanted to check out how bad it might be for Gaston in advance of Pelletier coming to interview him about the body that was found on Friday. He reminded me of something that happened when I was first posted here. You don't need to know the details. But what happened made me realise then that I hadn't dealt with the psychological effects of the incident in Paris properly, but I still did nothing about it. Yesterday, I finally had to admit to myself that I had to exorcise it from my mind. Back in 2007, why I ever thought that keeping my police revolver in the bottom drawer of my desk at the gendarmerie was enough and was all that I needed to deal with this… I just don't know. Another stupid decision!"

"No, Jacques. Not stupid, just the only way that you could handle this back then. That's all."

"Of all the cases I handled in Paris, that was the only one where I didn't get the arrest I wanted."

Jacques was hollow-eyed when he met Pelletier at the bar to interview Gaston. Later, at Ferme Pamier, he sat at the end of the large kitchen table and just listened to the discussion, taking notes throughout.

"We'd been hunting all day and we had a good bag at the end of it. It was when we were walking out of the forest and back to the vehicles that we found Juan."

"Can you pinpoint the exact spot?" Pelletier asked.

"Perhaps, all I can remember is that it was near the first set of stands, about forty, fifty metres in front."

"Would that mean that he would have been in the line of fire?"

"I would expect so." Pamier looked down and shook his head. "I don't know what we were thinking when we found him. But you'd just arrived, Jacques, from Paris and with all your procedures and need to do everything by the book." Pamier stared at him. "We didn't know you then. You weren't one of us; you didn't understand the village."

Jacques winced at the accusations. "Yes, there are a few things that I've realised over the last few days."

Pelletier glanced at Jacques, then turned his attention to the farmer. "Did no-one suggest calling the emergency services?"

"There was no point. I checked for a pulse; there wasn't one, and his body felt cold. He was dead. We all saw that he was dead."

"What time of day was it when you used the first set of stands?"

"Early, we were there from around four-thirty in the morning and started shooting at about five or just after."

"And the time when you discovered the body?"

Pamier shrugged. "I can't be sure, but it must have been about three, maybe four in the afternoon. It was starting to get dark and it was something glinting in the last of the sunshine that drew our attention to the body. If we had taken the west path we wouldn't have found it at all. And there have been so many times when I've wished that we had done that."

"We have a list of everyone in the hunting party from Gaston, but who was with you when you made the discovery?"

"Gaston was at the hospital in Mende with you, Jacques. The three men from Mende, that I didn't know well, were there, and the other party of six that we were with that morning had taken the other path."

"What happened then?"

"I told the three from Mende that they should leave it to us. I said he was a village boy and that we would deal with it. They went back to their vehicles and left, and I started running towards the village. I had no clear idea about what I was going to do next, but as I came down the road I saw Gaston driving up and flagged him down."

"Whose idea was it to conceal the body?" asked Jacques.

"Mine. It was mine alone. The trouble we had had in St Nicholas, the boy always turning up unexpectedly and following my wife around like a little dog, the rumours... I just thought we could be free of it permanently. It was me who persuaded Gaston to help, Jacques. He wanted to involve you and make the report, but not until the next day. I couldn't understand why he wanted to wait and he never explained. So, we just buried him behind the old farmhouse up on the north pastures."

"So Fermier Rouselle knew nothing of this prior to his discovering the body when he was reclaiming what he maintains is his land?"

"That's right."

"One last question, Monsieur, what weapons did you have with you at the time?"

"I always take four weapons. Three 16-bore shotguns and a 12-bore."

Pelletier looked at Jacques and they both stood and took their leave.

"A shooting accident, do you think?"

Pelletier strode on towards the bar where he had left his car. "Very probably. The victim's family say he was autistic and that his behaviour could be unpredictable, but that he would never harm anyone or any living thing. Being in the area of a shoot could have upset up him sufficiently so that he put himself in danger, I suppose. A murder charge? I can't see how I can make that stick at the moment, but I have other enquiries to make and there will need to be an inquest."

Jacques stifled a yawn. "Gaston also uses a 12-bore shotgun."

"And what weapons were you using?"

"None. I've never owned any weapons apart from my service revolver. I had the use of one of Gaston's 16-bore guns, but I never fired a single shot that day."

Pelletier smiled and pulling his coat around him got in the car and started the engine. "I'm glad to hear that."

In his office in the Vaux Investigations building in Mende, Jacques waited for Aimée to arrive. His examination of the work undertaken by Michelle and her team on the expenses indicated that she was possibly the only person within the project team that he could question to help him to understand the thinking behind the misappropriation. Checking his watch, he realised he had just enough time to make himself a coffee.

When he walked back to his desk, Aimée caught up with him just as his phone buzzed. It was a text from Philippe Chauvin. He decided he would look at it later.

"I want to talk to you about Hélène and the use of the Vaux Group credit cards. But I must ask you to be discrete about our conversation. I don't want anyone else on the team knowing what we are going to discuss today. Ok?"

Aimée settled herself and said, "It's alright, Jacques, I know when to keep my mouth shut."

"Do you know how this policy has come to be common practice within Édouard's team?"

"I'm not sure I can answer that. But when I arrived, as part of my induction into the company I had to work with Hélène and the admin team for a couple of weeks. I was told it would give me a good grounding in the current projects that we were handling, and it would be a good introduction to the rest of the workforce. It was already in place then and I questioned it. I'd never come across this before and when some expenses were presented to me to check, one of them being Hélène's, I asked her for an explanation."

"And what was her response?"

"I can't remember everything she said, but she did tell me that Édouard was happy for us to use the credit cards in that way and that all the directors did the same and something about… Oh yes, she didn't see why some of the junior members of the organisation couldn't have 'the same perks as the senior managers'. And then she made some comments about it 'only being fair', I think." Aimée frowned and then looked at the floor. "I can't remember anything else, sorry."

Jacques pulled out some stapled sheets of paper and started looking through them. "I've noticed that your claims are all in arrears and that you don't use the card in cash machines, so why did you not follow what the others were

147

doing?"

"Because it's not right, Jacques. The company pays for our travel in advance as part of a contract which means that we get subsidised train fairs for any travel we undertake in connection with work. But there is no similar contract with the restaurants in town. So, how is it possible to know what the bill will be? In addition, there are only certain things for which we can claim, and if a meal is offered with a quarter carafe of wine then we cannot claim for anything over and above that. How do you know in advance that you will want more than a quarter carafe? I think that people here are cheating on their expenses and getting away with it because the HR team are so stretched. It's just a way of giving yourself a pay rise."

"I notice that all your claims are weekly and completed every week without fail and fully supported by receipts."

Aimée let out a small gasp. "Of course, they are! It's the right way to do them."

"And you've never been tempted to just add a little extra here or there?"

"Absolutely not! What are you suggesting?"

Jacques smiled, satisfied that he'd got the right reaction. "Just doing my job, Aimée. I have to ask awkward questions."

"OK."

"Thanks, and I'll move on to something else now. You've worked with Hélène for a while and I just want to explore with you how she operates. When we first talked, a couple of weeks ago, you told me to watch for myself and to see what happens."

"Yes, I remember."

"I've done some delving since then, and I want to ask about Nicolas Durand and why he was interviewed under disciplinary procedures for what seems to me nothing more than a genuine mistake. It was the incident where papers were copied out—"

"That wasn't Nicolas' fault," she interrupted. "That was all Hélène. There was a high-level paper that had been drafted and needed to be circulated to senior managers only. Among other things, it covered the rationalisation of one of our clients' estate and therefore the potential for office closures. A list of possible sites to be considered for closure was included as an addendum. That addendum was only to go to certain individuals. So, there were two sets of copies needed. Hélène gave the complete document to Nicholas to copy. I was there at the time, and she never pointed out to him that only certain recipients should receive the addendum. Nicolas did as he was asked. But, before he started sending out the document I had read it and realised there was an issue. I told him to check with Hélène and to ask her directly if the addendum should go to everyone. He did ask but Hélène was very clever."

"What do you mean?"

"Nicolas asked the question specifically so that the answer should have been either yes or no. But she prevaricated. She asked him what instructions he had already been given. Nicolas answered truthfully and repeated what she'd said earlier. Then she made a snide comment. I can't remember exactly but it was something along the lines of 'so you do have a memory, Nicolas', or something similar."

"What happened then?"

"I got a call from Philippe Chauvin pointing out the mistake and quickly took action to get all the copies recalled. Unfortunately, it was too late for some of them and one or two leaked out to managers within the client's organisation. Next, the issue was raised at a management team meeting and, what amazed me was that, Hélène told a bare-faced lie. She said that Nicolas had acted without instruction and that she was taking appropriate action to make sure it didn't happen again."

"How do you know she lied in the meeting?"

"Because I was there and I heard her say it. I was so astounded that a manager of her status would lie in such a forum that I had to take a few moments to collect my thoughts. Naturally, Madeleine was at her snarling-tiger best in response."

"What happened then?"

"After the meeting, I warned Nicolas to be on his guard and when the minutes were issued I checked them carefully to make sure that there was no record of the discussion of the action of a junior member of staff. But it was there. All of it. His name, Hélène's response, everything!"

"And did you do anything about it?"

"I emailed Madeleine and said that I didn't think it was appropriate for individual staff performance issues to be recorded in the minutes in detail. I suggested that it would be sufficient to detail that a particular issue had arisen and was being handled. That's how I've always managed this sort of stuff or as part of a one to one discussion with my boss or the individual concerned."

Jacques threw his notebook down on the desk. "Why would anyone want to work in an organisation that was governed by fear?"

Aimée shrugged. "They don't. Would you?"

Jacques thought about his previous boss, Fournier, and their various, and mostly unresolved, disagreements when he'd been in the gendarmerie and compared that with his time in the Judiciaire in Paris. His relationship with Fournier had been toxic. *I made the right decision.*

He looked at Aimée. "I wouldn't want that either." He tapped his pen against the papers on his desk. "You seem to have a good grounding in management skills, Aimée. You've challenged others in the team, but I look around and I see a lot of stress and a lot of discord. Why is that?"

"I don't know, Jacques. There seems to me to be some sort of policy that underlines everything, it's just that only certain people know about it, and I'm not one of them."

wednesday, october 28th

Beth sat at the back of the tiny church. Every available space was taken by someone from the village or from nearby Rieutort. The funeral service concluded, Père Chastain led the way out of the church. The coffin, carried by the men of the village, followed with the principle mourner, Ricky Delacroix, head bowed and in respectful silence, behind. Slowly, the pews emptied and the procession moved in slow paced unison along the short and steep incline of Grande Rue to the entrance to the village. Beth glanced at the sign for the street name on the wall of one of the farms and couldn't help but question how little the length, breadth or nature of the road reflected the grandeur of its name.

At the tall iron cross, denoting the boundary of the village, the procession halted for one more prayer. Moving on, the coffin and Guy Delacroix's sole mourner, descended the further incline and entered the cattle tunnel to cross to the cemetery on the other side of the *route nationale*.

Beth, one of the very last, stared straight ahead as she followed Gaston, Marianne and everyone else. Footsteps echoed as they moved under the road and her black coat gently brushed against the white and green of the displays of flowers set in small arrangements along the length of the tunnel. The track on the opposite side of the road was uneven and stony. Treading carefully, the entourage climbed the 450-metre path to the tall wrought iron gate of the cemetery which guarded a small square of carefully tended territory belonging to the dead. Some of the oldest monuments were beginning to crumble and only the carved names of the more recently interred provided a clue to which family they belonged. Père Chastain led the coffin and mourners to a plot towards the centre where a large grey granite headstone declared the occupants of four previous generations of Guy Delacroix's ancestors.

The coffin in place, Père Chastain began his prayers at the graveside and Beth, her head bowed out of respect, let her eyes move across the names on the headstone. Guy, Francis, Guy, Bertrand, and their respective wives and some children. And then Émilie with a life span of just two days. Next was Clemence and the dates denoted that the mother had joined her child within the week. The name, probably the very last, to be carved next to it would be Guy Delacroix. Beth considered what the stone was telling her and dabbed a tear from each eye before they could reach fruition and roll down her cheeks.

The holy water cast into the grave and the final prayers intoned, Beth looked up as the principal mourner let some soil fall onto the coffin lid. Père Chastain concluded the service with the final petition and an awkward silence settled. The villagers began to move away and Beth was about to do the same when she realised that neither Gaston nor Marianne had moved. She waited and watched as the recently arrived Monsieur Delacroix let the single white lily he had carried throughout slip into the grave. Then he turned and slowly moved forward through the small crowd, which seemed to draw aside to let him pass without effort. As he drew close to Beth he looked straight at her and nodded, a half-smile crossing his face. Beth looked away and Monsieur Delacroix moved on until the procession was behind him. He kept on walking but, unlike everyone else who moved towards the Salle des Fêtes, he strode out along the D6. Reaching the sweeping bend close to her chalet, he disappeared out of sight, and Beth followed the rest of the village to the community room.

***

Through the transparent walls, Jacques could see

Madeleine was at her desk in her office. He noted that the door was closed when he arrived as arranged. He knocked and waited. And waited. Twenty minutes later, the door opened and Madeleine invited him in with her most gracious smile which he returned with one of his own.

"Jacques, take a seat and tell me what you need to know?" She took her place behind her desk.

"I've been checking the phone records for everyone in the company, and I've come across a couple of things that I just want to check with you." He pushed a small note across the desk containing a mobile phone number. "Do you recognise this number?"

She barely glanced at it. "No."

"That's odd, because there are several occasions when your business phone has been used to dial that number. Can you explain that?"

Madeleine, shrugged. "A mistake on the phone company's part, then."

"Hmm. I've checked the records for your personal mobile and that number has been dialled from that phone too."

"Has it? I can't imagine how that has happened. As I said, I don't recognise the number."

And there's that smile of yours again!

"I have a printout here that shows that they are text messages, Madeleine. So, who have you been texting recently?"

"I only text my own team and other colleagues as required."

He presented her with another sheet of paper that contained details of the calls to and from the number in question over the last month. "Look at this, and you'll see that on some days you apparently have whole conversations by text between you and the owner of the number in question. You must know each other quite well by now."

"As I said, Jacques, I don't recognise the number, and I would expect that the phone company have made an error. Was that all you wanted?"

"No. Fridays, I believe you have regular meetings in Rodez, is it?"

"What about them?"

"I was wondering what their purpose was, that was all?"

Madeleine smiled. "I was project manager on a contract for a client in Rodez. Both the contract and the work came to an end in January but I am providing voluntary on-going support to a particular manager over there on a one-to-one basis."

"So, this is contracted work?"

"On a voluntary basis, as I said."

"But if you are claiming expenses for the visits, even though your support is on a voluntary basis, there will still be a contract, won't there? And where would I find a copy of the said contract?"

"I wouldn't know, Jacques. Is there anything else?" She looked over to the door. "I've a lot of work to do so if you wouldn't mind closing the door on your way out."

Jacques grinned and got up. "You know, I'm surprised at you, Madeleine. There was a time when you would have said that a manager in need of this level of support for such a lengthy period is someone who is really not up to the job in the first place."

She made no response and he walked out, leaving the office door wide open. As he skirted round the first bank of desks on the way to his own, the door to Madeleine's office was slammed shut with such fierceness that everyone in the room looked up.

Jacques took his place in front of his own computer and grinned.

The large house on the outskirts of Mende, stood in its own grounds, and fitted Jacques' view of the kind of property that Édouard Vaux and his wife would share. The grounds were gated and the substantial property was fronted by pillars and a round tower at each corner with a traditionally styled and pointed roof.

The entrance hall, with its polished wooden floor, Indian

rugs, sweeping staircase, and extensive landing on three sides at first floor level, was surmounted by a large stained glass cupola above.

Madame Vaux, immaculately dressed in pale blue skirt and jacket and a fresh white blouse, greeted him warmly.

"We can talk in my study," she said, leading the way through a door just off to the left. The square room was lined with books and had a large antique partner's desk by the windows which looked out over the gardens at the back. Madame Vaux took a seat on one of the sofas that flanked the large fireplace and indicated that Jacques should sit opposite.

"I like a mint tea in an afternoon, Monsieur Forêt, would you care to join me or would you prefer something else?"

"Tea will be fine, thank you."

She poured the tea and passed Jacques an elegant china cup and saucer with decoration that perfectly matched the decor of the room.

"I wanted to talk to you about your time working for the Vaux organisation before you left to look after your children. I understand from Mademoiselle Lapointe that you were your husband's personal assistant for a while."

"That's correct. I joined the company – it was called Vaux Business Management at that time – in 1972 as a typist. I didn't work as Édouard's PA until the company was reconfigured into Vaux Consulting and Vaux Investigations in 1975."

Jacques made a note of the date and then produced the photocopy of the scrap of the letter. "Can you tell me anything about this, Madame Vaux?"

She looked at the page and read the text and then shook her head. "I don't think I've ever seen it before but I know what it refers to."

"Can you tell me about it?"

She handed the sheet back. "Before Édouard and I were seeing each other, he was accused of being the father of a baby to someone he had never met. There were a number of letters that came to the company address. I'm not sure

155

what's happened to them, but Édouard's mother told me about it. She decided that they all should be kept."

"Do you know where they were kept?"

"Are they not in the company files? That's where I would look for them."

"I will check. Can you remember what your mother-in-law told you about the matter."

Madame Vaux placed her empty cup and saucer on the tray. "She said the letters had come from a young woman claiming to have met Édouard whilst on a student exchange. She had subsequently found herself pregnant and was asking for help and support for the child. She was Catholic, so it was against her religion to have an abortion, and then, of course there was no morning-after pill. I believe the child was born and then given up for adoption, but we never heard anymore. I can't be sure, really, about what happened after that."

"And the name? Do you know her name?"

Madame Vaux shook her head. "I have no idea, but if you search the files you should be able to find out the details from the letters or ask Eloise. She should be able to find them for you."

"Eloise! You are must know Mademoiselle Lapointe very well to be able to address her as Eloise. She is most insistent in the office that we all use her surname!"

"She has always been very formal. Even when we were at the lycée together. She was always very—"

"Was that the lycée here in Mende?"

"Yes. She was in the year below me, but we were great friends and always have been. It was a great surprise for me at the time that it was my old friend from school that took my post when I left to have the children."

"Twins, I understand."

Madame Vaux got up and collected a framed picture from her desk. "Twin boys," she said, showing Jacques a photograph of them both in their caps and gowns. "Both with their own careers now, and one with his own family. I don't see them as often as I would like." She resumed her seat.

Jacques smiled. "Why was it a surprise that Mademoiselle Lapointe was appointed?"

"We lost touch after school. Eloise went travelling, I think, and I started work. And of course, when the applications came in for the post I didn't recognise the name. It was only when she turned up for the interview that we realised we knew each other."

"I see and can you remember what was her name when she was at school with you?"

"Yes. There are some things you never forget, Monsieur Forêt. It was Nowak."

"And now it's Lapointe, did she explain the change to you?"

"Not really. She said something about her mother wanting a more French-sounding name and I never really enquired."

"I see. Well thank you for your time and the tea and I'll see myself out."

As he walked back to his bike, Jacques wondered about the fragment of the letter. If all of the correspondence had been kept, as Madame Vaux alleged, then why put a fragment of a letter in a place that he would find it. *And why now?*

He put his helmet on and straddled the bike. *More importantly, who wants me to find this and for what purpose?* He shook his thoughts from his mind, started the engine and made his way back to his own office. He had some more checking to do and Eloise Lapointe was the target.

thursday, october 29th, 4.47am

The streets of Mende were deserted as a black-clad figure carrying a large rucksack took a left off Boulevard de Soubeyran, then turned into a quiet courtyard and halted at the corner of the building.

No lights. No sound. Just like before.

Cat-like, the figure moved silently across the courtyard, removed the rucksack and set it down quietly. Gloved hands removed a cloth and a knife from a jacket pocket. The cloth, soft and thick, was placed on the exterior sill. The knife began to work at the decayed putty around a pane of glass in the window. A strip of tape was taken from another pocket at the front of the jacket and the waxed paper backing carefully prised away as the tape was stuck from the centre of the pane up to the rib of the window and then further onto the pane above. The next three sides were treated in the same way. The knife was put away again and from a pocket in the black combats a slim pair of pliers were retrieved. The pins anchoring the pane in place were teased out one by one and placed side by side on the sill. One hand rested against the glass to keep it from falling. The other hand gently peeled the top piece of tape away, then the left and right and then, as the glass was controlled and allowed to come away from the frame, the final piece of tape was silently lifted and the glass was free, resting on the cloth. The pins were collected together and rolled into the corner of the cloth which was then wrapped around the pane and placed out of the way on the floor. The interior catch was opened and the two sides of the window teased open. The rucksack was lifted, passed through the opening and gently lowered to the floor. Two hands on the sill, body levered up, and the black-clad figure climbed into the room. *I'm in.*

The only light came from the street lamps at the front, filtered through the windows and the frosted glass of the door between the back room and the shop front. *Best keep down.* Two sidesteps right and into the corner by the window and Luciole was safe from prying eyes.

Corner of the room. That's best. Always the corner of a room. His hand reached out and felt the wall. *Dry. Very dry.* Steel grey eyes stared above. *Wooden beams. Perfect. I can change them. I can use them and I can destroy them.* He looked down. *Dust. Months and months of dust and bone dry paper.*

Working quickly, he unbuckled the rucksack and removed a flat-packed cardboard box. In seconds the box was opened up and placed in the corner of the room. He drew a set of matches and a rag from a front pocket on the bag. The rucksack was inverted over the box and dozens and dozens of packets of crisps were allowed to slip into the space to make a neat pyrotechnic pyramid. The dry rag was added at the apex. *Matches and then the burn.*

The first match lit immediately. Applied to the rag, and a dancing yellow flame appeared. A second match, another flame. And another. *Burn...* The steel grey eyes widened as the smell of the embryo fire was inhaled. *Burn...*

His feet on the window sill, empty bag in hand, and a single, silent jump to the ground outside. Windows pushed closed again and the pane of glass collected and stuffed in the bag. *Run and hide...*

Run but stay close enough to hear and smell the burn.

***

The pillar of smoke rising from the centre of Mende could be seen for miles. The acrid smell of burning filled the air. Beth stood at the end of the street. Gendarmes were in place to keep back the curious as the fire crews drenched the building. A number of other properties on either side had been evacuated and their inhabitants could now only watch and wait. Jacques recognised an ex-colleague and strolled across to speak to him for a moment and then returned.

"The seat of the fire appears to be at the back, but Gendarme Lefevre is going to ask one of the officers to talk to us at the next change-over of crew. There's nothing we can do. I've told him that we'll be in the café on Boulevard du Soubeyran."

"Monsieur Forêt?" The fire officer, his heavy protective clothing reeking of smoke, his boots leaving a wet trail on the floor as he approached, removed his glove and shook Jacques' hand and nodded to Beth. "I understand you have an interest in the property."

"Yes, that's right. I was about to take on the lease so that I could set up a photographic studio here. Luckily, although I've signed the paperwork, I haven't handed it over yet. But I was wondering what the damage was and how long it might take to repair?"

The fireman removed his other glove and helmet and sat opposite her. "I think you should look for another property. The fire started in the corner of the back room and spread up the walls, across to the window frame and over the ceiling. The wooden beams are badly damaged, part of the ceiling has come down, and there is some damage to the floor above as well as the consequent water damage."

"Was the fire deliberate, do you think?"

"I'm not really qualified to say, Monsieur Forêt, but, from what I have seen, I am certain there will be an investigation."

"Will it take long?"

"No, Madame, as soon as we have finished damping down, the building will be secured and another officer will undertake the investigation. Any conclusions will be reported to the police, the building owners and insurers, as appropriate. What happens after that will all depend on the conclusions of the investigation. If it is arson, there could be a lengthy police investigation. It's hard to say."

Beth smiled weakly and nodded as the fire fighter got up

and left. "Why would someone do this? And if the fire was started deliberately…"

"We don't know that yet." A cloud of suspicion drifted across his mind as he led Beth out of the café. He still didn't know who was behind the insidious notes that kept appearing on his desk in his absence. Whilst the content of these had not been directly threatening, they were certainly taunting. *Just one step away from a direct threat which is one step away from action.* He shook the thought from his mind as they walked in silence to the car.

***

At the back of the building another little crowd had gathered and was being held at bay by more *gendarmes* who were unaware that the fire starter had returned. Skulking in the shadows, Luciole looked out from under his favourite dark green hoodie that hid the black jacket. He had been there since the first fire crew arrived. The light in his grey eyes had not dimmed at all. The rapid breathing had barely slowed and the taste of burning was still in his mouth. When the wood slats in the walls and the beams in the ceiling had pyrolysed the taste had morphed from harsh melting polymers to the sweetness of oak mixed with pine and smoke. From his original hiding place, he'd heard the faint crackle of the flames as they moved over the walls, the tinkle of the remaining glass in the windows as it stressed and fractured in the heat. The piercing whine of the sirens had meant it was time to come out and watch.

Luciole was watching still.

***

"I'll work at home today," said Jacques as they let themselves in to the chalet. "I've got some digging to do and I can easily do that here."

Beth sank down on a stool at the breakfast bar. "I can't stop asking myself why? Why would anyone do that? What

161

have I done to make someone want to destroy someone else's property?"

Jacques took a deep breath. "Don't think like that…and if you want to know the truth, I don't think it's you that is the target, Beth. I think it's me."

"What do you mean?"

"I've been getting threatening notes at work. They started just after I began this investigation and they have continued. I think someone is feeling the pressure and torching the property you wanted to use is a tactic to stop me asking more questions."

"What are you going to do?"

Jacques sat down next to her. "I'm going to keep on investigating. I have to. I know from speaking to Philippe Chauvin that someone within the Vaux Group is actively working to destroy the company's credibility. I need to find that person and I will. And I intend to keep you safe. From today I don't want you going anywhere without me."

***

At her desk in the loft area, Beth began sorting through the box files of photographs that she had collected from Old Thierry. She stacked the files on the bookshelves in date order and then picked out the first one from May 1938. The contents were carefully ordered, dated and the subject of each photograph was detailed on the back. *This is going to be easy!*

An hour later and she hadn't been able to make up her mind which of the many shots to choose.

***

In the dining area Jacques was going through the phone records. The number that Madeleine had denied any knowledge of didn't come up on any of the other Vaux employees' statements. He dialled it and waited for it to be answered. It was just left ringing. Realising that he was using his company phone, he reasoned that the call might not have been picked up because the owner of the phone might have his number in their contacts list. He took out his personal mobile and dialled again. The call was not picked up. When he tried again five minutes later, the phone was switched off.

"Whoever you are, it appears that you only answer calls from a specific number. Hmmm…probably a pay as you go, I should think."

He picked up his phone and dialled another number. "Thibault, I need a favour… I need to trace a number… It's a mobile and yes, I do know that I shouldn't be asking you to do this for me, but I can give you a very good reason…" He read out the number and thanked his ex-colleague.

Returning his attention to the phone records, he realised that there was no printout for Eloise Lapointe. He rang Michelle in HR.

"I was wondering what had happened to the statement for Mademoiselle Lapointe's phone… Why doesn't she use one? … Has she never had a company mobile?" Jacques listened with incredulity. "Everyone has a mobile… So how does she keep in touch with the office when she's out?" He frowned. "And you're certain she doesn't have a personal mobile either… And if she is sick how does she inform you that she won't be in?" He listened as Michelle explained that Mademoiselle Lapointe had only ever taken three periods of sick leave during her time with the Vaux Group, and on each occasion her neighbour had telephoned to let them know. Jacques ended the call. *Eloise has no mobile phone!*

He sprinted up to the loft area. "Beth, I just want to run something by you. Mademoiselle Lapointe doesn't use a company mobile phone and according to Michelle in HR she doesn't use a personal one either. She has never submitted any claims for reimbursement of the cost of business calls. In addition, she has no landline at home."

Beth pushed her hair back behind her ears and thought for a moment.

"Maybe she doesn't want to be constantly contactable. Around the time Dan died, and just after, I switched my phone off and left it in a drawer. I just didn't want to talk to anyone at all. Perhaps she wants to keep her business relationships completely separate from her personal life. Is that really so strange?"

"No, I suppose not."

"There is another scenario, perhaps she does have one but only gives the number to specific people she wants to use it and work colleagues are not on that list."

"Hmm…" He sprinted back down the stairs.

All the work on the printouts finished and his notebook filled with follow-up questions, Jacques made a space on the dining table for his laptop. He set it running and used his remote log-in to access the surveillance camera footage from the previous day. He knew what he was looking for and he scrolled through to late morning and watched the screen. Half an hour later he paused the video and grabbed his notebook. "That's interesting. It would seem Aimée is right." He replayed it again.

surveillance camera footage

Hélène and Madeleine are in full view.

28/10/2009 11.27.04

"I'm not happy about Forêt delving into all the personnel files." Hélène shoves her hands into her coat pockets.

28/10/2009 11.27.18

"Just keep a cool head. I know how to handle Jacques."

"But you know he phoned my previous employers, don't you? He knows about the false declaration on my application for the job in Rouen."

28/10/2009 11.27.39

"It won't take him long to find out about the investigation in Paris that was being conducted against me because of an allegation of harassment and intimidation."

28/10/2009 11.27.52

"That investigation was stopped. I stopped it before I left."

"How can you be sure he doesn't already know about it?"

28/10/2009 11.28.13

"Knowing Jacques, he probably already does know about it. He'll be saving that little nugget for another day when he can unsettle you further."

28/10/2009 11.28.28

"But how did he find out, Madeleine, if you stopped the investigation?" Hélène casts Madeleine an angry look.

165

"There will still be the original paperwork, Hélène, which anyone with the right authority can access. It's not rocket science! Even you must be able to work that out?"

28/10/2009 11.29.07

Hélène, face in view, glares at her boss. "So, what else will he find?"

"Whatever's there. He's an ex-policeman, Hélène, and he won't stop until he has found every possible scrap of detail that he needs."

28/10/2009 11.29.22

"You need to keep your mouth shut from here on and think before you speak, and stop wasting my time."

28/10/2009 11.29.39

friday, october 30th

The hire car was a small hatchback, but comfortable enough. Beth was glad she had made the suggestion. Her car, with its English plates and right-hand drive, would have been too noticeable and would have easily drawn unwanted attention. They were parked in the public car park just to one side of the Vaux Investigations building. Here, Jacques had a clear view of the side road opposite that linked with Boulevard Théophile Roussel, which would be Madeleine's only access to her route to Rodez once she had left the underground car park of her own building.

"Make sure you get a clear shot of the car, including number plate and her driving as she comes out of the side street. With any luck the traffic will mean that she has to wait for a few moments."

"I'll do my best," said Beth. "Where are you expecting her to go?"

"According to her and the expenses claims she's been making she's going to Rodez, so she should take the first right off the ring road into Avenue Foch. But we'll see."

Beth looked at Jacques. He was watching the junction, never letting his attention waver. As the engine idled in readiness to follow Madeleine when she appeared, Beth wondered what she would look like.

"You've never told me much about Madeleine, you know."

Jacques glanced at her for a split second. "There's not that much to tell." His attention focussed on the junction again.

"But it is her, isn't it?"

"Yes. I'll answer anything you want to know later. Just

167

not now. That's her!"

Beth had her camera ready, lined it up and took one shot after another.

Jacques reversed out of the parking spot and moved towards the exit. Madeleine pulled onto the boulevard and immediately into the left-hand lane.

"Just as I thought, she's not going to Rodez." Jacques slotted into the same lane a couple of cars behind her. The traffic was beginning to get heavy in preparation for the lunchtime rush home. They moved slowly through the one-way system, onto Boulevard Henri Bourrillon and finally, out of the city centre on Avenue Père Coudrin and north on the N88 towards Langogne. Jacques kept well back and followed Madeleine through to Le Puy-en-Velay and an apartment block in one of the best suburbs in the city.

As soon as they pulled up, Beth was ready with her camera and caught Madeleine leaving the car, locking it and entering the building. Jacques was out of the car and following on foot. Beth kept her eyes on the entrance to the building.

A second car arrived and parked in a space next to Madeleine's. Following Jacques' instructions, she took shots of the car, the male driver who got out and continued to take photos as he made his way into the same building.

A few moments later, Jacques reappeared. "She took the lift to the sixth floor," he said as he got back into the driver's seat. He took his notebook out of his pocket and as he read the names from the eight mail boxes for that floor he rewrote them in print on a clean page.

"How do you know who she's visiting?"

"I don't, but I will when I've checked out who these people are and who is registered at each of those apartments on that floor."

Beth set her camera on the dashboard so that it was within easy reach should she need it. "There was a man who arrived just after Madeleine. He parked next to her and then went inside."

"I heard someone coming, and I ran up the first flight of

stairs and then came back down again. Did you get a shot of him?"

"Yes, I took a number of photos."

"According to the display above the lift door, he also went to the 6th floor."

"Does that mean something important?"

Jacques smiled at her. "It might. At the moment, it just means that he also went to the same floor. He may be visiting someone, or he may live here. I won't know until I check."

"Why do you never talk about her?"

Jacques ran his hands through his hair. "Because I don't want to." He began to fiddle with the fob hanging from the ignition key.

"Why?"

"For a long time, I thought she was the right person for me. But it didn't work out and I thought it was my fault."

"It's never usually just one person's fault."

"I'd been promoted and was anxious to impress my new team and my new boss. I was spending a lot of time working late at the office, and whenever an undercover operation came across my desk I took it and would then disappear for days and weeks at a time. I came back to my apartment one day after three weeks away on a case and she'd gone. She'd taken everything. Her clothes, CDs, everything. The place had been cleaned and it was tidy. So tidy, it looked like the estate agent's carefully dressed property to show to prospective buyers. It was almost as though she had never ever been there."

"Didn't she at least leave a note?"

"No. Nothing. Not even a forgotten piece of mail in the bottom of a drawer. I'd been spending too much time at work, and I hadn't paid her enough attention. I won't make that mistake again," he said as he took Beth's hand in his.

Beth frowned. "What did you do?"

"After I realised that she had gone, I tried to get in touch with her to ask her why. I kept leaving messages for her on her own phone and on her business number. I went to her office several times to try and catch her after work but she always managed to avoid me, somehow. Then, about three weeks later, she turned up at my place."

He pinched the bridge of his nose with forefinger and thumb and winced at the pain. "She came back to tell me that she had been seeing another man for over six months. I knew something had changed, but I thought it was just our relationship beginning to mature. I had no idea she'd met someone else. When I thought about it later I realised that she really didn't have to tell me that. She could have just said she'd had enough and left it at that. But she didn't. She made a point of telling me, and letting me know who he was."

"Did you know him?"

"I'd met him a couple of times at events that her company had hosted. He was another consultant that she came across regularly at business meetings, so I'd heard her talk about him quite a lot."

"Is that who she's meeting today?"

"The man who went into the building after her? I didn't see him."

Beth flicked forwards through the shots until she found the ones she wanted and showed them to Jacques.

"No, that's not him. That's Roger Baudin."

Beth looked over towards the apartment block in time to watch Madeleine and Roger leave, and picked up her camera. "Isn't that them?" She took a series of shots as they both returned to their cars and drove off in different directions. "Who do we follow now?"

"No-one," he said starting the car and shifting it into first. He shot her a sideways glance and smiled. "We go back to Messandrierre where I can focus all of my attention on you!"

toussaint – all saints' day,
sunday, november 1st, 12.00

The chill November air forced Jacques to pull up his coat collar as they crossed the car park to Pelletier's vehicle.

"So, you've known Aimée as a colleague for only a short time, but what can you tell me about her as a person? He said before he unlocked the car and got in.

Jacques took his place in the passenger seat. "As for Aimée as a person... She seemed quiet, intelligent and efficient to me. But..." He thought for a moment.

"Just say it, Jacques. We don't need to dance around each other." Pelletier reversed out of his parking spot and headed for the main road.

Despite the encouragement, Jacques detected an edge in Pelletier's voice and he took a few seconds to frame what he wanted to say.

"The dynamics between the team members seemed to me to be strained in some way. But I...I can't be precise about what the issues are. I haven't been included in all of their meetings, so there may be other pressures that I'm not aware of."

Pelletier checked his mirror before taking a right. "Pressures in relation to the project they were working on or personal pressures within the team?"

Reluctant to commit himself, but recognising that he would have to make a choice, he took a breath. "I'm not certain about this, but I think there could have been some personal pressure being exerted."

"By whom?"

It was a question of what to say next and he took a moment to decide. "By the team manager, I think. I know...

171

knew Madeleine Cloutier on a personal level in Paris. It didn't end well and I don't want to discuss the details. But she can be very manipulative. She is very adept at playing people off against each other." He sighed and shook his head. "There was a time when I thought that she was capable of anything. But that was a long time ago and... now I see that she is determined and still as ruthlessly single-minded as she ever was. She will do her job and do it very well, but it will be at the cost of any other people that she thinks will get in her way. What I think I may be seeing in her team is the result of her manipulating some individuals in order to get them to comply with her particular working methods and principles, which are not the same people management principles as my own. What I think I have seen is internal personal pressure being applied to certain team members. But Madeleine will have someone else she is using working in the background. I have some evidence of who that might be but I'm not absolutely certain yet, nor am I totally sure about how they fit in."

Pelletier nodded. "Someone for us to watch and interview perhaps?"

Jacques shrugged. "I don't know. I certainly don't think she's capable of murder, but I think it is entirely possible... that she could drive someone to perhaps..." He fell silent as his mind went back over the pathologist's report and recalled the single most important sentence that he had voiced only a couple of hours earlier. *Death by exsanguination from a wound to the left wrist.*

"Aimée was left-handed," he said. "It's definitely murder, because Aimée was left-handed." In his mind's eye, he was back in the room at Vaux, watching her as she wrote a short paragraph, signed it and passed it across to him to add to his evidence. "She was left-handed."

Eyebrows drawn into a tight frown, Pelletier parked up in silence. They both remained silent as they took a familiar route through to the morgue and the viewing room. The attendant carefully folded back the cover to reveal the face of the victim.

"That's not Aimée. It's Hélène Hardi," said Jacques.

In Pelletier's office, Jacques unpacked his laptop and set up the surveillance camera footage for the Magistrate to see. He set the video for Monday October 19th running and they watched in silence

"Go back to about 18.50," he said. "I want to hear that phrase she used again."

Jacques rewound the video and set it playing again. The Magistrate listened intently and then wrote down the phrase he was searching for. "Take it back once more, please." This time he let the section play through to its conclusion. "There's something you need to see."

Pelletier pulled out the evidence bag from his desk drawer that contained the piece of paper that had been found at the scene of the crime and showed it to Jacques.

"I know what you are doing," he read out loud. "Any fingerprints?"

Pelletier shook his head. "Could Aimée have sent that to Hélène, do you think?"

Jacques looked at the note again. "But why would she do that? She has already played her hand as you've just heard."

"Yes, but in the conversation on the video Aimée is saying that she knows that Hélène is trying to undermine her. What if Aimée knows something else?"

"If she did she never mentioned it to me." He thought back over the other conversations he'd had with her. "She told me about how she had been informed by Serge, the Head of Security, about the conversation between Madeleine and Hélène about her presentation style. Apparently, Madeleine demanded a meeting with her to discuss training needs. Aimée knew her qualifications were up to date, that she had passed her last consultancy exams with an excellent mark, coming second in her group of ten. She was surprised when Madeleine told her that there had been some comment from a couple of the other senior managers about her nervousness in handling presentations to the management board. At first, she was alarmed but then, as the conversation went on she realised that it was another manoeuvre by Madeleine and she just played along to start with. But when Aimée asked who had made the comments and why, Madeleine told her it didn't really matter, and that she needed to get some training to help her cope better."

"And what was Aimée's response to that?"

"She said that she would find out what worked best for her and deal with it. But the insidious undermining of Aimée has been going on for months from what she's told me… But there might be something else. The expenses – most of Madeleine's team are misappropriating company funds with Aimée being the exception. What if the letter was sent by Hélène to Aimée because she is not following suit and therefore drawing attention to the expenses issue?"

"It's possible."

"Aimée isn't the only one to receive taunting letters." Jacques retrieved his own correspondence and placed them on the desk.

Pelletier frowned and looked at the three letters together. "It looks to me as though they have all been created by the same person on the same equipment." Pelletier dropped each one in to an evidence bag and labelled them. "How did these come to you?"

"In the internal mail at Vaux. The third part of the puzzle is that a property that Beth was planning on renting was involved in a fire in the early hours of Thursday morning. I saw it as the action that was threatened in that second note."

"You'd better tell me everything else that you know."

"The cyber-attack at Vaux was from the inside. Philippe Chauvin has confirmed that the spurious code found on the network was introduced through one of the PCs in the reception area. He confirmed that by phone yesterday evening. I have yet to interview Madeleine Cloutier and Roger Baudin about their meeting in Le Puy on Friday. Considering the direction they each took after their meeting, I would have expected Madeleine to come back to Mende and Roger to go to his home address in St Julien. Yesterday,

174

I began checking the occupants and owners of the sixth-floor addresses of the apartment block they visited and as yet have found no link to Vaux. The trace on the mobile number that I asked for still isn't back, and perhaps we should expedite that. Eloise Lapointe has some gaps in her personal history that I still need to explore but Madame Vaux has given me a lead and I need to follow up on that. I haven't yet found the letters relating to the unknown child and I need to go through the old documents from Vaux."

"We'll work together on this, Jacques, from now on."

"There's some more video footage that you need to see," said Jacques as he clicked the fast forward button and took the footage to Thursday October 29th

surveillance camera footage

Madeleine paces backwards and forwards and continues to do so for two minutes and forty seconds. She stops as the grill begins to move.

29/10/2009 10.22.02

"You've kept me waiting." She glowers, face full to camera, as Hélène comes partially into view. "How dare you keep me waiting! When I tell you I want to see you I expect you to be here immediately."

29/10/2009 10.22.17

Hélène moves out of view. "I got here as soon as I could."
"Not soon enough. I'm waiting for an explanation."

29/10/2009 10.22.31

"I've checked and double checked everything on the F drive. The Communications Strategy is not signed off, Madeleine. It's not."

29/10/2009 10.22.48

"I don't know how Aimée can report to the board that it is. I've done everything you told me to do."

29/10/2009 10.23.06

"So how has this happened?"
There is silence for twenty-six seconds.

29/10/2009 10.23.39

"I don't know, Madeleine. I've done everything we

agreed. I know she's been spending a lot of time talking to Forêt. I can only guess that he's been helping her."

29/10/2009 10.23.55

"Have you spoken to her about the chats with Forêt and found out what they've been discussing?"

29/10/2009 10.24.17

"I've tried to get her to talk to me but she's been avoiding me, deliberately, I think."

29/10/2009 10.24.29

"Then you'd better do something about it. Go and see her tonight or first thing tomorrow morning. I don't care. I want her gone."

29/10/2009 10.24.42

"And what if she won't leave?"

"Sort it! I've been working on this for months and I'm not about to give up just because you can't do as you're told."

29/10/2009 10.25.03

"I told you Aimée had to go. I told you she was too clever to have on the team. I explained to you why she would be our greatest threat."

29/10/2009 10.25.17

"And look what's happened? I'm just about to make the final move and we've got Jacques examining everything we do. I told you to get rid of her months ago!"

29/10/2009 10.25.36

"But you can't even get that right, Hélène, can you? I sometimes wonder why I ever bothered to get you out of that first mess you got yourself into."

29/10/2009 10.25.48

Hélène moves into view. "Madeleine, we can still—"

"Just get out of my sight! I'll deal with this myself." Madeleine moves out of camera but does not go back into the building.

29/10/2009 10.26.07

monday, november 2nd

Pelletier and Jacques were seated and waiting in Madeleine's office when she arrived. She barely acknowledged Jacques and, taking her seat behind her desk, she focussed her attention on the Magistrate.

"We have some upsetting news for you, Madame Cloutier. I'm sorry to have to tell you that one of your staff, Hélène Hardi, has died."

Madeleine remained composed and stared straight ahead for a few moments. She turned her cold hard stare to the Magistrate. "How did this happen?"

"According to the pathologist's report, she was drugged with a concoction of sleeping pills and wine and then her left wrist was cut open."

"I see." Madeleine's face was calm and unreadable. "And when did this happen?"

"On Friday afternoon. Can I ask you were you were on that day, Madame?"

"I have a regular meeting with a client in Rodez. I left here at about eleven, and after my meeting I came back to Mende."

Pelletier glanced at Jacques.

"That's not quite true, is it, Madeleine?" Jacques took out his notebook. "At about 11.15 on Friday, you left the underground car park of Vaux Consulting and you drove to Le Puy-en-Velay where, at about 12.45, you met with Roger Baudin in this apartment block." He presented a copy of one of the shoots that Beth had taken. "That is you and Roger leaving at about two in the afternoon, isn't it?"

"And what has that got to do with you?" She scraped her hand through her hair and stared at the photograph.

179

"I also have CCTV footage of you and Hélène arguing that morning. In that conversation, you threaten another colleague, Aimée Moreau, and you encourage Hélène to go and see her that afternoon. Why did you do that, Madeleine?" Jacques waited for her response.

Pelletier let the silence drift for a moment before prompting her. "If you won't tell us about that then perhaps you can tell us what your meeting in Le Puy was about instead?"

Madeleine remained silent.

"Madeleine, I saw you leave Le Puy at about two," said Jacques, "and the direction you took would suggest that you returned to Mende. You would have been back here at about three-fifteen, three-thirty at the latest. Where did you go?"

"I went to my own apartment."

"And did you remain there?"

"Yes."

"Are you sure about that? In the same piece of CCTV footage that I've already mentioned, you tell Hélène that you are going to 'deal with this' yourself. What did you mean by that, Madeleine?"

"As you know, Jacques, I've been having some management issues with Aimée that I've had to resolve. She just isn't handling the work very well and I think what she really needs is to be regraded to a lower level so that she can gain more experience."

"That's an interesting re-interpretation of what has been happening, Madeleine," said Jacques. "From what I've seen and heard what you've actually been doing is intimidating a junior colleague."

"I sometimes have to take a hard line with staff in order to get the job done in the right way, Jacques. You know that as well as I do."

Jacques glanced at Pelletier.

"And when did you last see Hélène?"

"It was on Friday morning, Magistrate Pelletier."

"And you are certain of that?"

Madeleine nodded.

"Alright we'll leave it at that for the moment. I may need to talk to you again."

As they walked across the road to Jacques' building, Pelletier's phone rang and he took the call. When he hung up, he turned to Jacques, his face grim.

"There's another body – female – found by a dog-walker down by the river. You go and talk to Roger Baudin, and I'll deal with this and catch up with you later."

"Thanks for giving up your time, Roger. I need to talk to you about an incident that occurred on Friday."

Roger nodded his agreement and relaxed back in his chair. "Anything I can do to help, Jacques, as you know."

"On Friday, you met Madeleine Cloutier at an address in Le Puy. You were together for about an hour and a quarter. Can you tell me what that meeting was about and why it had to take place in Le Puy rather than here in the office?"

Roger straightened his tie. "I was wondering when you were going to stumble onto that. What has Madeleine told you?"

"I just want to hear what you have to say, Roger."

"Alright, Madeleine and I are seeing each other, and my wife doesn't know about it."

"I see; and how long has this been going on?"

"About a year."

Jacques nodded. "And do you always meet on a Friday?"

"Yes."

"And was it you who suggested that Madeleine continue to claim her expenses for these visits?"

Roger frowned. "I run the finances, Jacques, I would never suggest any such thing. If Madeleine is doing that, then she has done so without my sanction."

"You left Le Puy at about two on Friday. Where did you go?"

"I first went into the city to get some flowers for my wife and then I went home."

"Did you remain there?"

"Yes, and my wife came home at about six that evening."

Jacques flipped his notebook shut and placed a note in front of Roger. "That mobile number, do you recognise it?"

"Not really, but then I can't see the point of remembering numbers for mobiles because all the ones I need are in my contacts list."

Jacques pulled out his phone and began to dial. "So, if I ring this number…" They both heard the muffled ring tone of a mobile and Roger opened his desk drawer and took out his third mobile.

"That number is mine," he said as he placed it on the desk.

Jacques then presented the sheet detailing calls that he had presented to Madeleine. "Can you check your call history on that number for me, please. I'd like to compare it with this list."

Roger did as he was asked and handed the phone to Jacques.

"So, these are messages between you and Madeleine. That's a lot messages between you two just to manage a regular meeting on a Friday."

Roger glared at him. "We sometimes talk about work."

Pelletier removed his glasses and began to clean them as he updated Jacques.

"The second body is Aimée Moreau, Jacques. Initial findings from the pathologist at the scene are that she may have drowned, but there is a serious wound to her head. Estimated time of death… Predictably the pathologist didn't want to commit himself. I would suggest death occurred sometime between Thursday, when you last saw Aimée, and yesterday."

"How was the body not spotted sooner?"

"We think that she was hidden in weeds at the bank and the dog walker let his animal off the lead earlier than usual because there was no-one else around." Pelletier replaced his spectacles.

"A blow to the head and then pushed in the water, do you think?"

"It's possible. Her bag was in some undergrowth a little further downstream, but we still have not found the laptop and we do need her next of kin."

Jacques checked his phone to see if there had been a response to his call from the previous day. But there was nothing. "I'll follow that up."

"And what about your discussion with Roger Baudin?"

"He maintains that he and Madeleine Cloutier are having an affair. He has a mobile phone that he keeps just to contact her, he says. But I've checked the phone records, and there are a lot of messages that are passed between the two of them regularly. I think there's something else here, and I think it is connected with my internal investigation at Vaux. Someone is determined to discredit the company but who it is I'm still not sure. I'm also fairly certain that they are not working alone. The cyber-attack came from within the company, and apart from Philippe and his team, all of whom he has vouched for, there is no-one else with the relevant skills to mount such an attack. So there has to be someone else outside of the company who is involved."

"So how do you want to proceed?"

"I would like to see the CCTV footage for Aimée's building if you've got it. And the CCTV footage for the streets around where the fire occurred last Thursday. I'm sure there's a connection."

Pelletier nodded. "The Fire Investigator's report states the fire was arson and we have a team looking into the incident. We have examined that footage and we have two persons of interest that we are trying to identify. I'll give that team your number and get them to contact you. We've just received the footage for Aimée's building and I've got someone looking at that now. You're welcome to join them and let me know what you find."

The Vaux Investigations building was almost empty when Jacques returned to his desk late that evening. There was something he wanted to check against the surveillance camera footage that he had been looking at over the last couple of weeks. He pulled out the grainy grey pictures that had been printed out for him from the footage of the streets around the location of the fire and from the area around Aimée's building. Then he logged in to his desktop and accessed the secret drive on the network and re-ran the footage from the beginning. He let it run and never took his eyes off the screen until the time stamp for Monday October 19th clicked over to 16.49.03. He paused it and looked at the screen closely. He compared what he saw with the two sheets he had collected from Pelletier's team and smiled.

tuesday, november 3rd

"Beth, can you help me with something today?" Jacques poured her a cup of coffee and set it down on the breakfast bar.

"Will it take long? I wanted to do some more work on Thierry's book."

"I want you to go to the archives for me and check for some births, marriages and deaths. Mademoiselle Lapointe has some gaps in her history and I need to find out why. Her previous name was Nowak, and her date of birth is May 17th 1955. I also need to know if she had a child in 1971 or '72, whether she married at all, and to confirm that her mother died in 1985."

Beth stared at him wide-eyed. "Jacques, I know because of your job you have an amazing memory for information, but I need you to run those details by me again and only after I've got a piece of paper and a pen!" She moved across the kitchen and began searching through a drawer full of papers and envelopes and found a small notebook. "Right, I'm ready."

The birth in 1955 was easy enough to find and Beth noted the details and the parents' full names. The search for the birth in the seventies was proving tiresome. She'd begun in January 1971 and had worked steadily forward until lunch. She'd picked up the search an hour later and moved forward from November 1971 through to December 1972. There was no details that matched her search criteria.

Then she looked at the death records for 1985 for Madame Nowak senior, but found nothing. Going back to the beginning of the year, she searched again for the name of Lapointe and again her work was fruitless. She phoned Jacques.

"There's nothing… I've already searched twice under both names and there's nothing, Jacques… OK, I'll hang on here."

In Pelletier's office, later that afternoon, Jacques worked through some possible theories.

"This man has been seen in the vicinity of the property that was burned, Aimée's building, and we've now found him in the vicinity of some of the streets that lead down to the river close to where Aimée's body was found."

"That doesn't make him a murderer, Jacques."

"No, you're right, but he was in the right place at the right time on Friday when Hélène was killed."

"Why do you think Hélène was killed?"

"I don't know. She was instrumental in carrying forward some of the strategies that have been employed at Vaux to undermine personnel on the team. As yet, I can find no link between the discrediting of the company and her death, unless she knew too much and had to be silenced. But that's very tenuous."

"Why would anyone work to discredit the Vaux Group to such an extent that they may become bankrupt, Jacques? Why would anyone do that?"

"I've had that thought circling my mind for weeks. I've seen the tensions within the workforce, even between the two brothers, but I can't pinpoint who or what is behind it. I've even considered that one of the brothers is seeking to remove the other in order to gain absolute control, and that might be true, but why take action that means that the company loses business. It's that point that I keep coming up against."

Pelletier stood and turned to look through the window to the street below. "Can you apply any pressure to Roger Baudin, for instance, or Madeleine?"

"I can try, but I want to wait for the results of some searches that Beth is undertaking for me. There may be nothing useful but I'd still like to see the results."

"Alright, we'll leave it at that as I need to go back to Messandrierre this afternoon to talk to Fermier Pamier about the de Silva case."

"Something new on that one?"

"We've checked with the other members of the hunting party and none of them had a 12-bore shotgun that day. Or at least none of them are admitting it."

"So Pamier is in the frame, is he?"

"It would seem so."

***

Ricky Delacroix emerged from his meeting with the *Notaire* in Mende only twenty minutes after he'd arrived. Business had been swift and, as he suspected, there was very little of value in the estate except the house and land, and that would be his from now on. He had remembered what his father had always said about his brother being a hoarder and a skin flint, and Ricky wondered if there was more to find.

He walked to his hotel, packed his bags and paid his bill. An hour later, he was in Messandrierre and parked at his uncle's property. He unlocked the farmhouse door and went in.

The place was a mess. The wallpaper was old fashioned and peeling off the walls in places. The furniture in the main room was old and shabby, and there were papers and other bits of debris over every surface. He walked into the kitchen and recoiled at the smell. Back in the main room, he pulled open a couple of drawers on the large dresser that stood against the back wall. They oozed junk and detritus. He shook his head and slammed the drawers shut. Upstairs, he looked through the two bedrooms and found them in a similar condition. Finally, he went up into the roof space. The attic smelt of damp and when he moved to the gable end, he found an ineffective repair through which rain had leaked in. There were boxes filling every available inch of space.

He decided to check the possibility of renting a chalet again. At least, he'd be close enough to be able to go through everything and then get it cleaned and habitable again, and then he'd decide what to do.

***

Jacques joined Beth at the archives.

"I've done the extra searches you wanted," she said and passed a couple of documents across to him. "The only children I can find under the name Vaux are for Édouard and his wife. Twin boys."

"That confirms what Madame Vaux told me at least," he said. "Anything else?"

"Mmm. I think this might be what you're looking for."

Jacques took the copy of the details of a birth and a death and studied them. "That puts a completely different perspective on everything."

He took out his phone and called Pelletier.

"I've got a name for you to run a check on. And I'd like you to undertake some checks on a couple of bank accounts, too. Michelle sent me a text whilst I was on my way here to meet Beth. I've got Aimée's next of kin details… It's a brother who lives in Alès… Yes, that's right about two, maybe two and half hours away by train. Possibly, it's too far to commute on a daily basis but not long enough to prevent regular trips home at weekends for instance… Probably and we can check that when he is informed of the death… I'll be with you in a few moments." He ended the call.

"Thanks, Beth, this is good work. Go home and lock the door. I'll be there as soon as I can, but don't wait up for me."

wednesday, november 4th

The boardroom at Vaux Consulting was bathed in cool winter sunlight as Magistrate Pelletier and Jacques waited for all the attendees to arrive. Alain Vaux was seated on Jacques' right and had been punctual as always. Madeleine Cloutier, Philippe Chauvin and Roger Baudin had drifted in independently of each other. Édouard made an entrance ten minutes later and Mademoiselle Lapointe followed immediately behind.

"We've got a number of issues to deal with today arising from my internal investigation," said Jacques, "and I will take up as little of your time as I possibly can. Magistrate Pelletier is here because there are now two deaths connected with this case, and he will comment and add to the discussion as required." Jacques and Pelletier nodded to each other.

Jacques turned his attention to Alain Vaux. "You asked me to conduct an internal investigation into the apparent losses of business from Vaux to C and C Consulting. In the course of that investigation, I've come across a number of other things and I'll deal with those first."

He looked at Édouard. "Within your team, there is widespread abuse of the expenses accounts. You and Alain will need to decide how you want to proceed and whether you want to just seek repayment or pass the details to the police so that charges can be considered."

Jacques detailed the process and demonstrated how the credit card system had been used. He handed a file of papers over to Alain.

"Shouldn't those papers come to me so that we can take appropriate recovery action from salaries? Roger Baudin looked across at Alain.

"All in good time," said Alain. "I want to hear what else Jacques has to say."

"The project team are not the only ones who are guilty of misappropriating company funds, are they, Édouard?"

"What the hell do you mean by that?"

Édouard stood and was about to leave when Magistrate Pelletier spoke. "Monsieur Vaux, I would prefer it if you and everyone else remained in this room until Jacques has presented his case in full."

Édouard, jaw set, glowered at Pelletier but resumed his seat.

"With the help of the Magistrate Pelletier's team, I've had some bank accounts checked." He placed a copy of an account in front of Édouard. "There are regular payments from your account to Mademoiselle Lapointe. €500 a month. Would you like to explain what that is for?"

Édouard slapped his hand over the piece of paper and screwed it up. "How dare you?"

"Monsieur Vaux, we can handle this here as requested by your brother or we can move to my domain a few streets away. I would prefer you to answer the question here and now," said Pelletier.

Édouard thought for a moment, looked at his younger brother and said, "It's payment for a debt."

From Jacques' vantage point at the head of the boardroom table, he could see the changing expressions on everyone's faces as he had delivered that particular shot of information. Philippe Chauvin showed his disgust quite openly, Roger Baudin was as unreadable as ever, and Mademoiselle Lapointe remained composed and unfathomable.

"At that level of repayment, it must have been a very substantial debt."

Édouard made no comment.

Jacques then presented another sheet of paper to Édouard. "This is a copy of a record of a birth and—"

"We've been through this already. I've told you that

woman was a fantasist."

"I'm not talking about the letters from 1971, Édouard." He turned his attention to Mademoiselle Lapointe. "When we spoke last week, you gave me some details about your own background. But there were gaps and I couldn't understand why. When I checked your personnel file, I noticed that you had taken some leave in 1985. It stated in your file that your mother had died. But she was already dead by then, wasn't she? In fact, she had died in 1980 when you were twenty-five, and it wasn't her illness that forced you to come back to France, was it? It was her death. I looked at your file again and realised that the period of absence was for six months – and that could mean a number of things. In your case, it meant the birth your son Luc Vaux Nowak who was born in 1985, and that copy of the birth details shows that Édouard is the named father." A strained hush pervaded the room as Édouard paled and looked across at his PA.

"Mademoiselle Lapointe, would you like to add anything?"

A glimmer of a black look flitted across her face as everyone in the room focussed their attention on her.

"Yes, that is my son," she said. "And the money is for him, but I had no idea that it was coming from company funds."

"Would you like to tell us about your son?" Jacques waited for her response.

Mademoiselle Lapointe looked down and shook her head.

Magistrate Pelletier got up and moved over to the window. "I regret to tell you, Mademoiselle, that your son is in custody and has been since late last night." He turned to face her. "When did you last see him?"

"A few days ago. He wanted some money. He always needs money."

"And how do you keep in touch with him?" Pelletier moved further down the room until he was standing right behind her.

"I don't, he just turns up when he wants something and then he leaves again."

"He doesn't keep in touch with you by mobile phone, perhaps?" Pelletier glanced at Jacques who, under the cover of the table, dialled the number that had been taken from Luc Nowak's contacts' list.

"Is that your phone, Mademoiselle, that's ringing?"

Eloise Lapointe glared at Jacques and at everyone in the room. She then delved into her handbag and brought out the mobile and placed it on the table.

Jacques ended the call.

Pelletier moved back to the head of the table and stood beside Jacques. "Luc Vaux Nowak has a string of offences for arson and petty theft. I want to interview him about a fire in Montbel earlier this year as well as the incident here in Mende. Did you know he has a criminal record? And I would think very carefully before you answer that question, Mademoiselle. We have Luc's phone and we have seen the messages you have exchanged with each other over the last couple of weeks."

As Mademoiselle Lapointe remained silent, Jacques picked up the thread again. "To return to the internal investigation about security breaches and leaks of detailed information to a rival company. I used the help and technical expertise of Philippe Chauvin to follow through on some of that work. I'll let Philippe inform you all about what we found."

"Thanks, Jacques. I'll deal with the cyber-attack first. When we realised our protocols had been breached, our attention was to re-secure the network at all costs so that we could inform our clients that no further breaches would occur. We automatically assumed the attack was from outside the company and we missed some spurious code. When we examined that code in detail, we were able to trace its source. The code had been introduced onto one of the PCs in the reception area at Vaux Consulting. Both of these areas in each of the two Vaux buildings are covered by CCTV, but as the desks are constantly manned by Serge's

192

team during the time the offices are open there is no opportunity for anyone to introduce the code. But two days before the cyber-attack, Serge walked in to find that CCTV in reception at his office block had been turned off and then back on again a short time later. That's when the we believe the code was introduced. In the, aftermath of the attack, no-one thought to check the CCTV."

Philippe paused, poured himself a glass of water from a bottle in the centre of the table, then he continued. "Jacques provided me with a list of bids that he and Alain believed might have been tampered with after they were agreed and finalised. These were the bids that we had lost to C and C. We undertook a number of electronic audit trails on those documents, and we discovered that changes had been made to the documents before they were issued to the appropriate companies for consideration. Those changes were undertaken by you, Madeleine Cloutier, and by you, Roger Baudin."

Alain stared at his Finance director. "Why? Why did you do that? I've spent my life building this company and I thought we had the same goals. So why?"

"To redress the balance, Alain." Roger sneered as he looked across at his boss. "To redress the balance for my wife. She's the child mentioned in those letters from 1971. The child that no-one would acknowledge, the child that was adopted and moved from foster parent to children's home to foster parent for most of her young life." He looked directly at Jacques. "Those meetings in Le Puy. They weren't what you thought they were, Jacques. The admission of an affair was what Madeleine and I agreed to say should your snooping get to close to us. We were meeting a representative of C and C Consulting."

"And where are those letters now, Monsieur?"

"I've got them," said Mademoiselle Lapointe. "I needed them to use the detail to find Roger's wife. And when an opportunity arose for Roger to be recruited to the company, I took it. A little suggestion here, a nudge there, is all that it took. You see, Édouard, you may have been paying for your son for these last two years, but you never offered anything until I forced you to acknowledge him. When Madeleine joined the company, I knew then that finally we could put everything in place to get you out. We were planning to table a vote of no confidence in you at next month's meeting. But you ruined everything, Alain. You had to bring Jacques in to the company and you had to set him looking around, didn't you?"

"That's enough." Pelletier was on his feet. "Two lives have also been lost. Madame Cloutier. We have CCTV footage of you and Hélène Hardi entering Aimée Moreau's apartment block in Merle late on Friday afternoon. What happened?"

"They both had to go," Madeleine said, her voice harsh. "Hélène wasn't able to keep her mouth shut and was making too many mistakes. She was thinking for herself without consulting me too often, and she was putting everything we'd worked for in jeopardy. Aimée was a threat, too. She knew too much, and when Jacques arrived she was being influenced by him. Another month, and she would have left of her own free will. But you interfered, Jacques. You got in my way. She had to go."

"How did Aimée's body get from the apartment to the river?"

Madeleine scraped her hair back behind her ears. "I misjudged how much wine she'd drunk and whilst I was dealing with Hélène she left through one of the side doors. I had to leave through the front door so that it wouldn't look suspicious, and as I came around the side of the building I saw her staggering towards the path down to the river. I followed her and then she tripped on some undergrowth and fell. She hit her head and rolled into the water. I just left her there."

Madeleine turned to Jacques. "Satisfied now? Have you got all your answers, Jacques?"

The disdain in her look caused Jacques to shift his chair back a few inches from the edge of the table. He wondered how he could ever have thought that there may have been even a possibility of a future for them together.

"Just one. Where is Aimée's laptop?"

"I've got it!" She spat out the words. "I had to know what she was up to with you."

Pelletier placed his hand on her right shoulder and informed her of her rights before leading her away.

Jacques shook his head and followed a few moments later. Once alone on the stairs, he pulled out his phone and called Beth.

saturday, november 7th

The morning was bright and Beth positioned her tripod in front of the porch and set the time lapse function on her camera. She moved back inside and poured herself a coffee from the pot on the stove, opened the bag of croissants that Jacques had left on the breakfast bar, and settled down to eat and enjoy the newspaper. A couple of hours later, and Beth was still slumming in the kitchen in her pyjamas and dressing gown. She checked the clock on the wall. "Oops, better get showered and dressed." She cleared away the pots, washed up and disappeared up to the bedroom.

A little later, she came back out onto the porch and checked her camera. The weak winter sun had moved round, the shadows had changed and she clicked the camera back to manual. As a matter of habit, she checked the focus and reset the picture, as she always did, even though she had no intention of taking any more shots. She disconnected the camera form the tripod and moved all her equipment inside and up to the loft area where she had been sorting through Old Thierry's files and photographs.

She put the camera in its bag, returned the tripod to its usual place in the cupboard and went back to her task. She had no real idea of exactly what it was that she was looking for. But Jacques had suggested that if she could find some photographs of the village from November 2007, she might be able to help him solve a problem. She kept searching and eventually came across a series of negatives that Old Thierry had stored in the box file labelled 'Hunting Scenes'. She used her desk light to view them and gradually worked her way through strip after strip until one particularly caught her attention. It wasn't the photo itself that made her stop and look again. It wasn't an especially interesting or scenic shot. It was something about the lines in the photograph that offended her eye's sense of order. She stopped and looked again. Still unsure of what it was she thought she had just noticed, she picked up her phone.

"Jacques, it's me. I know you're with Magistrate Pelletier, but can you talk?"

"Just a minute."

Regardless of his need for her to wait she continued anyway. "There's something odd I've found in Thierry's photos. I think you need to see it. When will you be back?"

She could hear Jacques speaking in muffled tones to Pelletier and then he came back on the line.

"OK, Beth, I'll be with you in about an hour."

She ended the call and arranged everything so that Jacques could look at the relevant negatives as soon as he returned.

"Beth!" Jacques burst in through the front door and sprinted up to the loft. "Let me see what you've found."

"Why is it so important, Jacques? They are not even very good shots. I think Thierry was shooting anything that moved that day or else he'd set his camera on the tripod on his time lapse setting and then forgotten to stop it when the light changed."

"Beth, this picture, negative or whatever, might help Fermier Pamier from facing a manslaughter charge. Can I have a look at what you've got?"

Beth switched on her desk light and held the negatives up in front. "It's the third one along. There's something not quite right with the lines in the photo. Look here, this one is at odds with the others."

Jacques peered at the tiny oblong of film. "Can you improve this or print it?"

"I can try running it through the scanner and then through my software to get it to look right. Just give me a few minutes."

Beth worked carefully and swiftly and the picture

197

appeared on her computer screen.

Jacques scrutinised the scene. "Can you zoom in on this section?"

She did as she was asked.

"That's Pamier, That's Gaston and there… Let's look at the next shot and the one after that." He pointed to the screen. "Zoom in again, please."

Beth did so and Jacques looked at the revised shot. "And that's de Silva. Zoom out…"

Jacques gasped. "Thierry, old man, you just don't know what you've done!" He pulled Beth to her feet, and held her tight and kissed her. "Beth, you've just saved an innocent man from a serious charge."

"But I don't understand, Jacques." She repositioned the picture on the screen and frowned.

"We know that figure there is de Silva," he said, standing behind her and pointing to a cowering figure in centre towards the back. "These are the stands, and that is Gaston and on his left is Pamier. If you look at the angle of the guns, you'll see that Pamier's is pointing up and out of the picture to the left. In the next shot Gaston has turned round to face the camera, Pamier is reloading his gun but de Silva is now standing."

Beth peered at her screen and nodded.

"Go to the last shot and you can see Pamier is holding his gun over his arm and breached. But in background de Silva looks as though he's falling. Can we get these shots printed?"

"Of course, but I'll have to take it to Mende, and it will take a few days."

"A few days, a week, it doesn't matter," he said.

sunday, november 8th

Ricky Delacroix woke at his usual time at an address in Mende that he neither owned nor rented. The blonde beside him was still asleep, and, he decided, she hadn't been worth the effort. Not caring whether he disturbed her or not, he got up, showered, dressed and walked out without a word, making sure he slammed the door as he left.

Back at the chalet in Messandrierre, he changed into jeans and a designer shirt, set out his breakfast and the newspaper he'd bought in Mende and opened his laptop, logged on and began checking his various investments and accounts. Everything in Ricky's world was running smoothly and a wide grin crossed his face.

Some time later an alarm on his phone interrupted his third cup of coffee and reminded him that he had booked a table for lunch at the restaurant in the village. Carefully picking out a jacket, he put it on and smoothed back his hair in the mirror. He grabbed his hat and coat and set out on foot for the delights of lunch in a small place half-way up a mountain.

***

In the chalet, Beth was working on her photographs from the day before when Jacques appeared at her desk.

"Hey, do you have to work so much?"

"I thought you were working on your formal report for Alain."

"I was, but I keep distracting myself, and there's something I want to ask you."

Beth saved her work and put the laptop lid down.

"Alright, I'm listening."

"I was wondering, if you're staying until Christmas, perhaps we can go to Paris for the holidays. You can meet Papa and my sister and the boys, and maybe you'll let me take you to a jeweller's I know in Montmartre and—"

"Jacques, we can go shopping…" Beth gave him an odd look. She half laughed and then frowned. "Are you?" She looked away. "Did you just ask me…"

Jacques grinned at her. "A yes would be nice."

THE END

Fantastic Books
Great Authors

CROOKED
CAT

Meet our authors and discover
our exciting range:

- Gripping Thrillers
- Cosy Mysteries
- Romantic Chick-Lit
- Fascinating Historicals
- Exciting Fantasy
- Young Adult and Children's
  Adventures

Visit us at:
www.crookedcatbooks.com

Join us on facebook:
www.facebook.com/crookedcatbooks

Made in the USA
Columbia, SC
06 June 2017